Criminal lawyer and bestselling mystery author Erle Stanley Gardner wrote close to 150 novels that have sold 300 million copies worldwide. Today, the great Gardner tradition continues with many of his classics back in print, as well as brand-new additions to the ever-popular series starring the incomparable Perry Mason.

By Erle Stanley Gardner
Published by Ballantine Books:

The Case of the
Rolling Bones

Erle Stanley Gardner

BALLANTINE BOOKS • NEW YORK

A Ballantine Book
Published by The Ballantine Publishing Group
Copyright © 1939 by Erle Stanley Gardner
Copyright renewed 1966 by Erle Stanley Gardner

www.randomhouse.com/BB/

ISBN 0-345-32979-1

This edition published by arrangement with William Morrow and Company, Inc.

Manufactured in the United States of America

First Ballantine Books Edition: December 1985

10 9 8 7 6 5 4 3

Cast of Characters

PERRY MASON—His methods raised objections in court, but they got results

DELLA STREET—Not only Mason's Girl Friday but all the other days of the week

PHYLLIS LEEDS—Niece and confidential secretary of wealthy old Alden Leeds

ALDEN LEEDS—He left the Klondike with gold in his pockets and something on his conscience

EMILY MILICANT—Alden Leeds's December heartbeat

NED BARKLER—Salty old prospecting pal of Alden Leeds, with an eye for the girls

PAUL DRAKE—Head of the Drake Detective Agency, he always looked disinterested and so succeeded in fooling the public

L. C. CONWAY—When Alden Leeds made out a $20,000 check to him, the whole case began

GUY T. SERLE—He bought Conway's crooked-dice business only to have the police raid his joint

MARCIA WHITTAKER—A beautiful blonde, hard as nails but soft about Conway, she cashed the controversial $20,000 check

JOHN MILICANT—To some he was known as Emily Milicant's brother, but others knew him under a different name

JASON CARREL—He took Uncle Alden for a ride and committed him to a sanitarium

FREEMAN LEEDS—He hadn't seen his brother Alden in fifty-three years but was quick to recognize him when he found out that Alden had come home rich

Chapter 1

Perry Mason stared at the morning mail with evident distaste. He raised his eyes to where his secretary was standing at his elbow, and said, "Gosh, Della, can't you scare me up a good mystery?"

Della Street said, "I've handled all the routine mail. This is the important stuff which needs your personal attention."

Mason pushed the mail to one side. "Shucks, Della, I hate letters. Letters are inanimate. I like people. People are animate. I like to puzzle with human problems."

Della Street regarded the discarded mail with solicitous eyes, and steeled herself against the magnetism of Mason's boyish grin. "After all," she said, "you can't eat dessert all the time, Chief. You have to have some bread and butter."

"Not dessert, Della," Mason said. "I want meat, red meat, and lots of it. Come on, be a good girl, and tell me about the clients."

Della Street sighed. "A Miss Leeds, a Miss Milicant, and a Mr. Barkler are waiting in the outer office. They're together, but Miss Leeds wants to talk with you for a few moments before you see the others."

"What's it about, Della?"

"A rich man whose relatives want his money."

"I don't like rich people," Mason said, pushing his hands down in his pockets. "I like poor people."

"Why?" she asked, her voice showing her interest.

"Darned if I know," Mason said. "Rich people worry too much, and their problems are too damn petty. They stew up a high blood pressure over a one-point drop in the interest rate. Poor people get right down to brass tacks: love, hunger, murder,

1

forgery, embezzlement—things a man can sink his teeth into, things he can sympathize with."

"I told them I thought you wouldn't be interested," Della Street said, "that you specialized in trial work."

Mason sunk his chin on his chest and frowned thoughtfully. At length, he said, "I'll see Miss Leeds anyway. She has my curiosity aroused. Three people come together. One person wants to see me before the other two. . . . Send her in, Della."

Della Street looked pointedly at the pile of mail.

"I'll answer it this afternoon," he promised. "Let's see Miss Leeds."

She slipped through the door to the outer office to return in a few moments with a young woman whose quick, nervous step was indicative of an impatient temperament.

"Phyllis Leeds," Della Street said.

Miss Leeds crossed rapidly over to Mason's desk, giving the lawyer an impression of vivid blue eyes which studied him in swift appraisal.

"Thank you so much for seeing me, Mr. Mason," she said as Della Street withdrew.

Mason bowed. "Sit down," he said. "Tell me what it's about."

She sat down on the extreme edge of the big leather chair across from Mason's desk, and said, "I can only keep the others waiting a minute or two. I want to give you the sketch."

Mason opened his office humidor, extended a tray containing four of the better-known brands of cigarettes.

"Smoke?" he asked.

"Thanks," she said. As Mason held his match, she took a deep drag, exhaled streaming smoke from her nostrils, then, with a quick, nervous gesture, whipped the cigarette from her lips, and said, "I want to see you about my Uncle Alden—Alden E. Leeds."

"What about him?" Mason asked.

"I have two cousins and two uncles living. Uncle Alden was the black sheep of the family. He ran away and went to sea when he was only fourteen. No one knows where he went or

2

what he did. He doesn't like to talk about his adventures, but he's been all over the world. When I was fifteen, he came back here to settle down. I think the family were inclined to look down their noses at him until they found out that Uncle Alden was exceedingly wealthy."

"How old is your Uncle Alden?" Mason asked.

"Seventy-two, I believe. He was the oldest of the boys. I'm living in his house, manage most of his financial affairs, and his correspondence."

"Go on," Mason said.

Phyllis Leeds said, "I'll have to hit the high spots. Uncle Alden has never married. Recently he met Emily Milicant. . . . She's waiting in the outer office. He fell for her hard.

"The relatives are furious. They're afraid they'll lose out on the money. They want to have Uncle Alden declared incompetent."

"And how do *you* feel about it?"

"I feel that it's Uncle Alden's money and he can do with it just as he pleases."

"You're friendly with Emily Milicant?"

"Not particularly."

"But you'd be glad to see them married?"

"No," she said, "I don't think I would, but I *do* want Uncle Alden to be free to do what he wants."

"And what," Mason asked, "did you want *me* to do?"

"Isn't it the law that a person can manage his own property unless his mind becomes so affected that other people can take advantage of him?"

"Something to that effect," Mason said.

Phyllis Leeds said, "They're trying to show that he *can* be imposed upon, and there are certain things they must never find out."

"What for instance?"

She said, "That's what I want Emily Milicant to tell you. But before she told you, I wanted you to—well, get the sketch. I think she wants to marry Uncle Alden. You'll have to make allowances for that. Ned Barkler is one of Uncle Alden's closest friends. He knew Uncle up in the Klondike years ago. I asked him to come along."

"Shall I ask them to come in?" Mason inquired.

"If you will, please."

Mason picked up the telephone, and said, "Ask Miss Milicant and Mr. Barkler to come in, please." He dropped the receiver into place and glanced expectantly at the door to the outer office.

Emily Milicant had quite evidently tried to preserve the contours of youth although she was somewhere between forty-five and fifty-five. She had starved her face into submission, but her body was more obstinate. Despite the hollows under her cheekbones and the wide intensity of her staring, black eyes, she retained little rolls of fat just above the hipbones. Dieting had made her face gaunt, her neck almost scrawny, but the fit of her dress across the hips lacked the smooth symmetry which she had so evidently tried to achieve.

Barkler was in the late fifties, weatherbeaten, wiry and hard. He walked with a slight limp. Mason acknowledged introductions, motioned them to chairs, and waited.

Emily Milicant dropped into a chair and immediately seemed to become thin. Her black eyes, staring out from above the hollowing cheeks, conveyed the impression of an emotional intensity which was burning up her mental energy.

Barkler took a pipe from his pocket with the manner of a man who intended that his contribution to the conference was to be an attentive silence.

Emily Milicant's eyes met those of Mason with the force of physical impact. "I presume," she said, "that Phyllis has told you all about me. It was delicate and tactful of her, but entirely unnecessary. I could have covered the situation in fewer words. So far as the Leeds family are concerned, Mr. Mason, with the exception of Phyllis here,"—and she indicated Phyllis by rotating her forearm on the elbow and twisting the wrist quickly as though to shake a gesture off her fingertips,—"I'm an adventuress. I have ceased to be known as Emily Milicant. I am referred to as 'that woman.' "

4

Mason nodded noncommittally.

"That's quite all right, Mr. Mason," she rushed on. "I can take it. But I'm not going to be pushed around."

"I think," Mason said, "Miss Leeds has covered the preliminaries. What is the specific point on which you wanted my advice?"

"Mr. Leeds is being blackmailed," she said.

"How do you know?" Mason asked.

"I was with him day before yesterday," she said, "when his bank telephoned. Alden—Mr. Leeds—seemed very much disturbed. I heard him say, 'I don't care if the check is for a *million* dollars, go ahead and cash it—and I don't care if it's presented by a newsboy or a streetwalker. That endorsement makes the check payable to bearer.' He was getting ready to slam up the receiver when the man at the other end of the line said something else, and I could hear what it was."

"What was it?" Mason asked.

She leaned forward impressively. "The cashier at the bank, I suppose it was, said, 'Mr. Leeds, this young woman is flashily dressed. She's asking for the twenty thousand dollars in cash.' 'That's the face of the check, isn't it?' Leeds asked. The voice said, 'I beg your pardon, Mr. Leeds. I just wanted to be certain.' 'You're certain now,' Alden said, and slammed the telephone receiver back into place.

"When he turned away from the telephone, I think he realized for the first time that I had heard his end of the conversation. He seemed to hold his breath for a moment as though thinking rapidly back over what had been said at his end of the line. Then he said to me, 'Banks are a confounded nuisance. I gave a newsboy a check for twenty dollars last night and put an endorsement on the check that would enable him to cash it without any difficulty. And a bank underling has to start acting officious. You'd think I didn't know how to run my own business.' "

Phyllis Leeds entered the conversation. "When Emily told me about it," she said, "I realized right away what a dreadful thing it would be if Uncle Alden had been victimized by

5

swindlers or blackmailers. Uncle Freeman would pounce on it at once as an excuse to show that Uncle Alden couldn't be trusted to handle his own money."

"So what did *you* do?" Mason asked.

"I went to the bank," she said. "I handle Uncle Alden's financial matters—keeping his bank account in balance and his correspondence and things like that. I told the bank I was having trouble in my accounts and asked them to give me the amount of Uncle Alden's balance and the canceled checks. I think the bank cashier knew what I was after, and was really relieved. He got the checks for me at once. The last one was a check for twenty thousand dollars signed by Uncle Alden, and payable to L. C. Conway. It was endorsed on the back, 'L. C. Conway' and down below that appeared in Uncle's handwriting, 'This endorsement guaranteed. Check to be cashed without identification or further endorsement.'"

"The effect," Mason said, "being virtually to make it a check payable to bearer. Why didn't he do that in the first place?"

"Because," she said, "I don't think he wanted this young woman's name to appear on the check."

"It was cashed by the bank without her endorsement?"

"Yes. The bank cashier insisted on her endorsing the check. She refused to do so. Then he rang up Uncle Alden and had the conversation Emily overheard. After that, the cashier told this woman she didn't need to endorse the check, but that she'd have to leave her name and address and give a receipt before he'd let her have the money."

"Then what happened?"

"The girl was furious. She wanted to telephone Uncle Alden, but she either didn't know his number or pretended she didn't. The cashier wouldn't give her Uncle Alden's unlisted number. So finally she wrote her name and address, and gave him a receipt."

"Fictitious?" Mason asked.

"Apparently, it wasn't. The cashier made her show her driving license, and an envelope addressed to her at that address."

Mason said, "Your uncle might not welcome the cashier's activities."

"I'm quite certain that he wouldn't," she said.

Emily Milicant said, with quick nervousness, "You know blackmailers never quit."

"You have the check?" Mason asked Phyllis Leeds.

"Yes." She took the canceled check from her purse, and handed it to Mason.

"What," Mason asked, "do you want me to do?"

"Find out about the blackmail, and if possible get the money back before the other relatives can find out about it."

Mason smiled, and said, "That's rather a large order."

"It would be for most people. You can take it in your stride."

"Have you any clues?" Mason asked.

"None, except those I gave you."

Mason turned his eyes to Barkler who sat smoking placidly. "What's your idea about this, Barkler?" he asked.

Barkler gave his pipe a couple of puffs, removed it from his mouth, said, "He ain't being blackmailed," and resumed his smoking.

Phyllis Leeds laughed nervously. "Mr. Barkler knew Uncle Alden in the Klondike," she said. "He claims no man on earth could blackmail him, says Uncle Alden's too handy with a gun."

Barkler said, by way of correction and without removing his pipe, "Not the Klondike, the Tanana."

"It amounts to the same thing," she said.

Barkler seemed not to have heard her.

"He and Uncle Alden stumbled onto each other a year ago," Phyllis explained. "They're great friends—old cronies, you know."

"Cronies, hell! We're pards," Barkler said, "and don't make no mistake about Alden. He ain't being blackmailed."

Phyllis Leeds said quietly to the lawyer, "The check you hold speaks for itself."

Mason said, "If I take this case, I'll need money—money for

my services, money for investigation. I'll hire a detective agency and put men to work. It'll be expensive."

Barkler took the pipe out of his mouth and said, "Cheap lawyers ain't no good anyhow. Alden ain't being blackmailed, Phyllis. He's in trouble of some kind. Give Mason a check and let him go to work. . . . But it ain't blackmail. You can lay to that."

Phyllis Leeds opened her purse and took out a checkbook. "How much," she asked Perry Mason, "do you want?"

Chapter 2

Paul Drake, head of the Drake Detective Agency, relaxed all over the big, leather chair in Mason's office. His backbone, seeming to have no more rigidity than a piece of garden hose, bent forward until his chin came close to his knees. His feet were propped against the opposite arm of the chair. He habitually sat sideways in the big chair, and adopted an attitude of extreme fatigue. His eyes were dull and expressionless, his voice had a tired drawl. His appearance of general lassitude and lugubrious disinterest in life kept anyone from suspecting he might be a private detective.

Drake said, "Give me a cigarette, Perry, and I'll tell you the sad news."

"Get it?" Mason said to Della Street, tossing the detective his cigarette case. "The big moocher comes in here and bums my cigarettes to report that he's foozled a case."

"Nuts to you," Drake said, extracting a cigarette and snapping a match into flame. "I did some good work on that case. The blonde who cashed the check gave the name of Marcia Whittaker. Her address checked with the address on her automobile license—but it wasn't her address. However, the name was right, and it didn't take me long to locate where she'd been living."

"*Been* living?" Mason asked.

"Sure," Drake said. "She hadn't figured on having to give her name at the bank. When the cashier demanded it, she was smart enough to give him the right name so it checked with her driving license. She was also smart enough to go home, pack up her things and move out that afternoon."

"Any back trail?" Mason asked.

"Of course not. What the hell do you think she moved for?"

"And that," Mason said sarcastically, "represents the result of your complete investigation, I take it."

Drake was silent while he drew in a lungful of smoke, then blew it out, and resumed his account as casually as though he had not heard Mason's comment. "I did a little snooping around the place where she had her apartment. The banker had described her as hard. That was only the first half."

"You mean hard and fast?" Della Street asked.

"You guessed it," Drake said. "So I hunted up the landlady and ran a blazer on her about the kind of joint she was running and scared her into convulsions. She said she'd do anything she could, but the girl hadn't left any forwarding address and all that. I told her I wanted to know something about the men who had called on Marcia Whittaker. That lead didn't pan out. Then I asked the manager if she gave apartments to every tramp who showed up without asking for references. She said she certainly didn't. She usually asked for references, although she admitted that if a girl gave references that sounded all right and didn't hesitate or 'hem and haw' about it, she seldom wrote to the references.

"So we looked up Marcia Whittaker and found that when she'd taken the place, she'd given as a reference an L. C. Conway, manager of the Conway Appliance Company at 692 Herrod Avenue."

Mason lit a cigarette. "Not bad, Paul."

"Just luck," Drake said, wearily. "Don't give me any credit for that—although you'd have been the first to blame me if the name hadn't been there. Anyway, it was a lucky break. I went down to 692 Herrod Avenue. The Conway Appliance Company had had an office there for a couple of months. It had received lots of mail, and then it had moved out suddenly and left no forwarding address.

"I got a description of L. C. Conway." Drake pulled a notebook from his pocket, opened it, and read, "L. C. Conway, about fifty-five, around five foot ten, weight a hundred and ninety pounds, bald in front, with dark, curly hair coming to a point about the top middle of his head. Has a slight limp, due to something wrong with right foot. . . . No one knew where he lived or what he did."

Mason frowned. "Couldn't find a thing?" he asked.

"Nope," Drake said, "but I found one thing that was significant."

"What?"

"The day after he moved, all mail quit coming to the office."

Mason studied his cigarette thoughtfully for a moment, then said, "Meaning a forwarding address had been left at the post office?"

"Yep."

"Any chance of getting it?"

"None whatever," Drake said, "but I bought a post office money order for twenty-five bucks payable to the Conway Appliance Company, scribbled a note that it was in payment of the merchandise I'd ordered a couple of months ago, and asked him to send it by mail to a phony address. I sent it to 692 Herrod Avenue."

"How did you know what kind of merchandise he was selling?" Mason asked.

"I didn't," Drake said, "but a guy like that isn't going to turn down twenty-five bucks, and he isn't going to take a chance on cashing a post office money order without giving the sucker some sort of run for his money."

Mason nodded. "Good work, Paul. Get an answer?"

"Yep," Drake said, squirming around sideways so that he could get his left hand into the inside pocket of his coat. "Found out what the bird's selling all right and got his address."

"What's he selling?"

"Crooked crap dice by the looks of things," Drake said, pulling a letter from his pocket and reading. "Dear Sir: It is our policy to make deliveries by messenger and never through the mail. Your valued order received, but you neglected to state whether you had any preference in color or size. Unless we hear from you to the contrary, we will deliver two pair of our regular ivory cubes. There will, of course, be the usual premium."

"How's it signed?" Mason asked.

"Signed 'Guy T. Serle, President,' " Drake said.

"Address?" Mason asked.

"Uh huh. 209 East Ranchester."

"So then what?" Mason asked.

Drake said, "Thought I'd drop in for instructions. Think I'd better let him make a delivery?"

"Yes," Mason said, "and tail the man who makes it. Try and pick up Conway and put a tail on him. Find out who Serle is."

Drake said, "Okay, Perry. Of course, this delivery guy will probably be a rat-faced punk who thinks he's a big shot because he's peddling phoney dice, but he may lead to something. I'll . . ."

He broke off as Mason's telephone shrilled into sound.

Mason said, "All right, Paul, be seeing you. Keep me posted," and picked up the receiver. The girl at the switchboard said, "Miss Leeds on the line, says it's a matter of the greatest importance."

Mason said, "Put her on," then, cupping his hand over the mouthpiece, said to Drake, who was halfway to the exit door, "Stick around a minute, Paul. This is the Leeds girl calling now. . . . Yes, hello. . . . Yes, this is Mr. Mason, Miss Leeds."

Phyllis Leeds was so excited that her voice was high-pitched. "Mr. Mason," she said, "the most *terrible* thing has happened."

"All right," Mason said, "let's have it."

"Jason Carrel, one of the relatives, has put Uncle Alden in a sanitarium and won't tell me where it is."

"How did that happen?" Mason asked.

"He called early this morning to take Uncle Alden for an automobile ride. When they didn't come back within an hour, I got worried. Uncle Alden doesn't like long rides, and I don't think he likes to ride with Jason anyway. I went around to Jason's house. Sure enough, his car was in the garage. I asked him where Uncle Alden was, and he said that Uncle Alden had

12

been taken very sick while they were riding and that he'd rushed him to a sanitarium and called a doctor, that the doctor had insisted upon absolute rest and quiet for at least two days. He said he was just coming to tell me about it when I arrived."

Mason said, "All right, I'll fix that in short order. Now listen, this is more important than it sounds. Does your uncle love to gamble?"

"Why, no, not particularly."

"Does he ever shoot craps for large stakes?"

"Why, no . . . well, wait a minute. He was in a little game a few days ago—oh, maybe a week ago."

"With whom was he playing?"

"John Milicant."

"Related to Emily?" Mason asked.

"Yes, he's her brother."

"How much did the brother lose?" Mason asked.

"I don't know. I think he won."

"How much?"

"I don't know. There was a little talk back and forth, a little kidding."

"Was the game for high stakes?"

"No—just twenty-five cents a throw or something like that. I don't know much about how to play the game."

"Where can I find John Milicant?"

"I don't know just where he lives. I can find out from Emily."

Mason said, "Get him. Bring him into the office. I want to talk with him. Don't worry about your uncle. I'll get out a writ of *habeas corpus* and serve it on Jason Carrel."

"And there's nothing else for me to do?"

"No."

"Nothing I can do to help Uncle?"

"Not a thing," Mason said. "Bring in John Milicant and forget about it. Quit worrying."

He hung up the telephone, said to Paul Drake, "Okay, Paul. It's nothing important. The relatives are closing in on the old man, that's all. Go ahead and get busy on the Conway Appliance Company."

13

As Drake left the office, Mason said to Della Street, "Get out a petition for a writ of *habeas corpus*. I'll present it to Judge Treadwell and we'll give Jason Carrel a jolt right between the eyes."

Chapter 3

When Mason and Della Street returned from lunch, Paul Drake had already returned and was waiting for them.

"What's new, Paul?" Mason asked.

Drake said, "We've located Marcia Whittaker."

"Good work, Paul. How did you do it?"

"Oh, just a lot of leg work," Drake said wearily. "We covered the Bureau of Light, Water and Gas. She had an application in for electric lights and gas. It's an unfurnished flat. She's evidently buying furniture and settling down."

Mason lit a cigarette and stared at the match for a long moment before shaking it out. "Marcia Whittaker's this girl's real name?" he asked.

"Yes. Why?"

Mason said, "As I get her character from your report, she's a drifter. Now she gets a flat and starts buying furniture. What's brought about this sudden stability?"

Drake hugged his knees. "Her split out of twenty thousand bucks."

Mason slowly shook his head. "That would send her on a splurge, not make her settle down. . . . Della, take a look at the papers—vital statistics. Just a chance, but maybe . . ."

The two men smoked in silence.

A few minutes later there was a triumphant grunt from Della. "This what you want? 'L. C. Conway, 57, to Marcia Whittaker, 23.' Notice of intention to wed."

Drake slumped down dejectedly. "Oh—oh," he said. "Here I thought I'd done something smart, when all I'd have had to do was sit in my office and open the newspaper. . . . Just another case of the professional being trimmed by the gifted amateur."

15

Mason grinned. "Anything more about Conway, Paul?"

"Nothing that helps. That twenty grand evidently made quite a difference to Conway. He sold his business to Guy T. Serle and gave Serle the right to keep on using the name of Conway Appliance Company."

"Does Serle know where Conway is?"

"I don't know. Look, Perry, what do you think of these?" He drew a pair of dice out of his pocket and threw them across the desk.

Mason looked at the dice, picked them up and rolled them three or four times, then laughed. "I'm ashamed of you, Paul," he said.

Drake said seriously, "That's the merchandise delivered to me by the Conway Appliance Company. Two pair of loaded dice, and a very special premium."

Mason shook his head, slid open a desk drawer and threw the dice in it.

"What do you think the premium was, Perry?" Drake asked him.

"Marked cards."

"No, a nice lottery ticket."

Mason whistled. "You tailed the delivery?"

"Sure. He chased around to twenty or thirty addresses, then beat it back to the East Ranchester address. I picked up Serle—a guy about forty, nervous, quick-moving chap, six feet tall, pretty slender, bony features, pinkish blonde, gray-eyed, wears double-breasted suits. I put a tail on him to see if he has any contact with Conway. . . . However, we have a cinch now. We can locate Conway by putting a shadow on the girl."

Mason pinched out his cigarette with swift decision. "I'd rather talk with the girl than with Conway," he said. "Della, when Phyllis Leeds calls, tell her Judge Treadwell has issued a writ of *habeas corpus*."

"Why did you pick Treadwell?" Drake asked.

Mason grinned. "He has an arcus senilis."

"What's that?"

"One of the things psychiatrists like to pounce on in senile dementia cases. You'll hear plenty about it in a day or two. Come on. Let's go."

Driving out in Paul Drake's car, Mason said, "The way I figure it, Paul, I'm retained by Phyllis Leeds. I'm not working for Emily Milicant."

Drake flashed him a sidelong glance. "Go on," he said.

Mason lit a cigarette. "A word to the wise," he said.

"I'm supposed to read your mind?" Drake asked.

Mason nodded.

They drove in silence for several blocks, then Drake turned a corner and said, "This is the place—any particular angle of approach?"

"No," Mason said, "we'll have to pick up the cards and decide how to play our hand when we see what are trumps."

They rang the bell twice, then heard steps on the stairs. The door opened. A blonde, attired in gold and brown lounging pajamas, stared at them with evident disappointment, and said, "Oh, I thought you were the man with the drapes."

Mason said, "Miss Whittaker?"

She said, "Yes. Now don't you boys tell me you're working your way through college."

"We want to talk with you," Mason said.

"What about?"

"About a private matter."

As she continued to stand blocking the doorway, Mason added significantly, "Something which I think you'd prefer to discuss where the neighbors couldn't hear."

She glanced at the doors opening on the porch. "Come in," she said.

Drake closed the door behind them. Marcia Whittaker silently led the way up the stairs.

The living-room had shades but no drapes. New rugs were on the hardwood floors. The furniture seemed stiff and unreal as though it had not as yet become accustomed to its new surroundings and settled down to homey comfort.

"Sit down," she invited tonelessly.

Mason studied her face, the yellow hair with a darker fringe

17

at the roots, her hard, blue eyes containing a hint of fear, her skin seeming smooth enough when her face was in repose but showing hard little lines which sprang into existence between her nose and the corners of her mouth as she placed a cigarette in her lips, adeptly scratched a match along the sole of one of her Chinese shoes, and said, "All right, let's have it."

Mason said, "It's about that check you cashed."

"My God," she said, "can't anyone cash a check without being hounded to death? You'd think I was the only person in the city who ever had a check to cash. I was a fool for giving my address. I found out afterwards I didn't have to."

"What was the consideration for that check?"

"None of your business."

"The point," Mason said, "is that this check was given by a man seventy-two years old who is now confined in a sanitarium."

"That's too bad," she observed without sympathy.

"His relatives will appoint a guardian if they can," Mason said, "and when the guardian is appointed he'll demand *all* the papers. When he gets the papers, he'll find that canceled check. Naturally, a guardian wouldn't like anything better than to start making trouble about that check. It would give him a lawsuit, attorney's fees, extraordinary compensation."

"What trouble could he make," she asked, and then added significantly, "for me?"

"Lots," Mason said.

"Leeds didn't give that check to *me*," she said hotly. "I only cashed it."

"You have the cash," Mason said.

"No, I haven't."

"You're marrying it, then."

She glared at him, said nothing.

Mason, studying the expression in her eyes, said, "Why won't Conway marry you?"

She flushed hotly. "Say, who cut you in on this deal?"

"I did," Mason said.

"All right. Since you want to mess around in my private affairs, why *doesn't* he marry me?"

18

Mason studied the end of his cigarette. "Do you think he ever intended to?"

"Of course, he intended to. He'd promised it all along, and then his family . . ."

She broke off abruptly.

Mason said, "Well, if you ask me, I don't think his family have any right to put on airs. You're just as good as they are."

"Say," she said abruptly, her eyes narrowing, "how do you know all this?"

Mason said, "Oh, I get around."

"Who are you?"

"The name's Mason."

"Who's the guy with you?"

"His name's Drake."

"Well, what's your racket?"

"Believe it or not," Mason said, "we don't have any. I thought I'd let you know about that check. Of course, Phyllis knows all about it."

"Oh, she does, does she?"

"And Emily," Mason observed.

For a split second, all trace of color left the girl's face. Her eyes darkened with apprehension. "Emily knows about it!"

"Yes, Emily Hodgkins," Mason went on.

Marcia Whittaker conveyed the cigarette to her lips, sucked in a deep drag, exhaled, tapped ashes from the end of the cigarette into the ash tray, and said, "Emily Hodgkins?"

"Yes, an assistant employed by Phyllis Leeds."

"Oh!"

"You don't know her?"

"I don't know any of them."

Mason said, "Your boy friend might be about twenty thousand bucks ahead if a guardian *wasn't* appointed."

She looked down at her Chinese slippers for several seconds, then raised her eyes to Mason, and said frankly, "Okay, I get you."

"It'll be too bad if your boy friend has a leaky face," Mason said.

19

"I get you. I get you," she said impatiently, "You don't need to embroider the edges."

Mason, getting to his feet, said, "Nice place you have here. Going to make a cozy little home."

Sudden tears sprang to her eyes. "For Christ's sake, don't rub it in! I've tuned in on your program. You haven't given your commercial yet, and I suppose you're not going to. Now that you're finished, why not get the hell off the air?"

"Thanks," Mason said. "I will."

She followed them as far as the head of the stairs. Her mouth corners were twitching. Tears were trickling down her cheeks, but she stood slim, straight, and defiant, watching the two men through the outer door.

As they walked across the street to the car, Mason said, "Judging from the way that banker talked, and your comments about her record in the apartment house, I thought we'd find a red light burning over the door."

"Remember," Drake said, "I was only taking the evidence of the people who had the apartment next door and the landlady who ran the joint."

"All right," Mason said, "suppose they *were* right? This kid's young. Conway wanted to use her in that check business. The way he sold her was by promising to marry her when he made the stake."

"Think he strung her along for the check business?" Drake asked, easing the car into gear.

"Of course, he did," Mason said.

"How about his family?"

Mason said, "There *may* be something there."

"Why all the agony over just cashing a check?" Drake asked. "That doesn't amount to so much."

"That," Mason said, "is our most significant clue. It amounted to a hell of a lot in *this* case."

Phyllis Leeds and John Milicant were waiting in Mason's reception room when the lawyer returned to his office.

John Milicant, a baldish, black-haired, stocky man in the
20

fifties, walked with an almost imperceptible limp—a slight favoring of his right foot. He shook hands, sat down, crossed well-creased, gray trousers, consulted his wrist watch and said, "Phyllis said you wanted to find out something about Alden Leeds. I'd appreciate it very much if you could rush things. I have an appointment I'm stalling off."

Mason said, "You understand there's going to be a family row?"

Milicant nodded. "Of course, Alden is right as a rivet. He's a little peculiar at times, just a little eccentric. He's no more crazy than I am."

"You've had an opportunity to observe him during the last few weeks?" Mason asked.

"During the last month mostly," Milicant said. "I drop in once in a while."

Phyllis interposed. "Uncle Alden gets a great kick out of John. John's about the only one who can give him a good fight over the chess board."

Milicant said, "I don't know whether he and Sis are going to hit it off or not. I don't care. It's up to them. I hope Sis has enough gumption to have it understood she'll never touch a cent of his money. She doesn't need it."

"You mean you'd like to have him leave it to the relatives?" Mason asked.

Milicant said, "If I were in his shoes, Phyllis would get everything."

"Have you shot any craps with him lately?"

"Yes. Sunday, I believe it was."

"High stakes?" Mason asked.

"A two-bit limit. But if you made a pass, you could let it ride and keep on building up."

"Would you consider it was being too personal if I asked you how much he won?"

Milicant said, "He didn't win. I won somewhere around a hundred dollars, enough to get a suit of clothes. But he seemed to get a great kick out of losing."

"I think it was because he was getting entertainment,"

Phyllis Leeds said. "You know, John, you keep up a running fire of comment."

Milicant laughed. "Well, I was always trained to talk to the dice. You can't expect them to do anything for you if you don't tell 'em."

Mason said, "Just a moment. I want to find out about some papers. If you can wait just a moment, Mr. Milicant, I won't detain you over five minutes."

Milicant was again regarding his wrist watch as Mason strode across the office, entered the law library, and then detoured through the corridor door to Paul Drake's office.

Mason nodded to Drake's secretary, raised his eyebrows in silent interrogation, and pointed toward Drake's private office. She nodded, and Mason went on in to find the detective sitting in his little cubicle, his feet on the desk, reading a paper.

Mason said, "Paul, I'm damned if I know whether this is just a hunch or whether I'm naturally getting suspicious of my fellow men. John Milicant is in my office. He's around fifty-five, about five foot ten in height, fairly stocky, wears good clothes, bald on top, and has a slight limp."

Drake frowned, and said, "What are you getting at, Perry?"

"Read that description again—the one that you have of L. C. Conway."

"I get you," Drake said. He pulled out his notebook, glanced through the description and said, "It fits. Of course, Perry, it would fit a lot of men."

"I know," Mason said, "but it's worth a play. Milicant will leave my office in about two minutes. Do you have an operative you can put on his tail?"

"I'll have a man on him when he leaves," Drake promised.

Mason returned to his own office, said, "I wanted to look up a matter. I won't need to keep you any longer, Mr. Milicant."

Milicant crossed over to shake hands with Mason. "If there's anything I can do," he said, "don't hesitate to call on me."

"I won't," Mason said, and then to Phyllis Leeds, "How are you making it?"

Her face showed hard lines. There were puffs under her eyes.

"All right," she said. "It would be a lot better if I thought Uncle Alden was all right."

"He's all right," Mason said. "Some doctor has him under opiates right now. That *habeas corpus* is going to scare them into the open. How's Barkler getting along?"

"I don't know. He isn't there. I don't know where he went."

"When did he leave?"

"Early this morning."

"Say where he was going?"

"No. He's peculiar. He comes and goes as he pleases."

Mason said, "All right. Go on back home. Try and get some rest. Take it easy. This is just preliminary skirmishing. Save your energy for the main fight. When we have that *habeas corpus* hearing, keep Emily Milicant out of the picture. I don't want her to seem too interested."

"Why?" John Milicant asked.

"Judge Treadwell might think she was waiting to sink her hooks into Leeds as soon as the court freed him," Mason said.

"I get you," Milicant nodded. "That's good advice. Come on, Phyllis. I have to rush to keep an appointment."

Chapter 4

Judge Treadwell's courtroom was well crowded. Phyllis Leeds, seated within the bar, looking ill at ease, returned Mason's reassuring smile with a nervous twist of the lips.

She indicated that she wanted to whisper to him, and Mason bent down so his ear was close to her lips. "Why all the people?" she asked.

Mason said, "Newspaper notoriety, money, romance, and a fight. People flock to that combination like flies to a honey jar. . . . Now can you give me a line on the other relatives without seeming to point them out?"

"I think so," she said. "That's Jason talking with the lawyer now. The man seated back of him is Uncle Freeman."

Mason sized them up, and said, "Your Uncle Freeman looks like an opinionated cuss."

"He is," she said. "When he once gets an idea in his head, you can't blast it out with dynamite."

"We'll let Judge Treadwell do a little blasting," Mason said.

"Jason's just as bad," she said, "only he's more clever. He's a mealy-mouthed hypocrite who always tried to make Uncle Alden feel he loved him—taking him for auto rides and all that. . . . There's Harold Leeds, Freeman's boy—the one walking on tiptoe. He does everything that way around home. When he can break away, he'd like to be a real sport; but he doesn't stand much chance. Freeman keeps him under his thumb, won't let him have a car, doesn't approve of . . ."

She broke off as the bailiff suddenly pounded the courtroom to its feet. The door from chambers opened, and Judge Treadwell, walking with slow dignity, marched up the three carpeted stairs to the platform at the end of the courtroom and took his

24

seat behind the mahogany "bench." The bailiff mechanically intoned the formula which announced that court was in session, and, a moment later, Judge Treadwell looked down at Perry Mason, and said, "I'd like to ask a few questions of the applicant."

Mason, on his feet, nodded toward Phyllis Leeds. "Stand up and be sworn, Miss Leeds," he said. ". . . walk right up to that desk. Did Your Honor wish to have counsel examine the witness?"

"No," Judge Treadwell said. "The court will ask the questions. How old are you, Miss Leeds?"

"Twenty-three," she answered in a voice high-pitched from nervousness.

"And your uncle is living with you?"

"Yes—that is, he was. I keep house for him, and keep his books."

"Now, I'd like to know something about the family," Judge Treadwell said in a conversational voice. "Your uncle, I take it, is not married."

"No, Your Honor. He's always been a bachelor."

"Tell me about the family."

"There's Uncle Freeman, a younger brother of Uncle Alden, his son, Harold, and Jason Carrel."

"Jason is the son of a sister?" Judge Treadwell asked.

"Yes, Your Honor. She's dead. She was the youngest in the family—that is, of the sisters."

Judge Treadwell asked kindly, "How do you get along with your uncle, Miss Leeds?"

"Very well," she said, "but anyone would get along with him. He never loses his temper, is kind, courteous, and considerate."

"And how about the other members of the family?" Judge Treadwell asked. "How do they . . ."

Opposing counsel was on his feet. "Your Honor," he said, "I dislike very much to object to the court's question."

Judge Treadwell turned to him. "Don't do it then," he said.

"I feel that in the interests of my client I must."

"You're representing Freeman Leeds?"

"Yes, Your Honor, Freeman Leeds, Harold Leeds, and Jason Carrel."

"What's the ground of your objection?"

"That this is simply an application for a writ of *habeas corpus*. The petition alleges on information and belief that Alden Leeds is being detained against his will. I propose to show that such is not the case. The man is in the custody of loving relatives, under medical care which is an urgent necessity."

"You'll have your opportunity," Judge Treadwell said, calmly. "Right at the present time, the court is trying to find out something about the family affairs and the general situation of the parties."

"I understand, Your Honor, and that's what I object to. I claim that is incompetent, irrelevant, and immaterial and not a part of this hearing."

"Objection overruled," Judge Treadwell said, and then, as the lawyer remained on his feet, observed mildly, "If you have any other objections to make, make them, and the court will rule. If you have none, sit down."

The lawyer sat down.

Judge Treadwell turned to Phyllis Leeds. "How about the other members of the family?" he asked. "How do they get along with your uncle?"

"Same objection," opposing counsel snapped.

"Same ruling," Judge Treadwell said calmly.

"Why, they get along with Uncle all right—that is, they did until—until Uncle Alden—I hardly know how to express it."

"Made outside friends?" Judge Treadwell asked.

She nodded her head vigorously.

"I think that's all," Judge Treadwell observed. "I notice that the petition alleges that Alden Leeds was taken for an automobile ride by Jason Carrel, and failed to return. I think I'll ask a few questions of Mr. Carrel. Come forward please."

Jason Carrel, a thin young man in the thirties with high cheekbones, close-set eyes, and a mop of coal black hair which grew low on his forehead, came forward and was sworn.

"From reading the return to the writ," Judge Treadwell said, when Carrel had stated his name, age, and residence to the clerk, "I understand you took your uncle for an automobile ride."

"Yes, Your Honor."

"What did you do with him?"

"I took him to a sanitarium when he exhibited symptoms of . . ."

"You're not a doctor?"

"No."

"Did you ask your uncle if he wanted to go to a sanitarium?"

"No, I thought . . ."

"Never mind what you thought. The question was whether you asked your uncle."

"No. I didn't think he was in any condition to give an answer."

"He was conscious?"

"Oh, yes."

"You were talking with him?"

"Yes."

"And did he make any objection to entering the sanitarium?"

"Yes, he did."

"And how was the objection overcome?"

"Well, I stated to the doctor that . . ."

"That's not the question," Judge Treadwell interrupted, kindly but firmly. "How was his objection overcome?"

"Two male nurses carried him in."

"I see," Judge Treadwell observed in the tone of finality. "I think that's all."

"Your Honor, I have a showing I'd like to make," the lawyer for the relatives said. "I feel that I'm entitled to . . ."

"Go right ahead with your showing," Judge Treadwell announced. "Court will hear any witnesses you care to produce— you have Alden Leeds in court?"

"No, Your Honor."

"The court order was that you produce him here."

"We understand, Your Honor, but he is physically unable to attend. We have Dr. Londonberry, who is here to testify on that point."

27

"Very well," Judge Treadwell said, "let him testify."

Dr. Londonberry was in the middle fifties, inclined to flesh. His complexion was ruddy, his gray eyes cold and professional, but his manner was plainly nervous. As he took the witness stand, he adjusted nose spectacles from which hung a wide, black ribbon.

Judge Treadwell leaned forward to appraise him, while the doctor was being qualified as an expert, then settled back in his chair with an air of complete detachment.

"You are acquainted with Alden Leeds?" the lawyer asked.

"I am."

"When did you first see him?"

"When he was brought to my sanitarium in an automobile driven by Jason Carrel."

"That was the first time you had seen Alden Leeds?"

"Yes."

"Now we won't ask what Jason Carrel told you. We only want to know what you saw and what you did. Please tell the court exactly what happened."

In the precise, clipped voice of a professional man who is prepared for a grueling cross-examination, Dr. Londonberry said, "I was called to the automobile. I found a man approximately seventy-two years of age, somewhat frail in physical appearance, and apparently suffering from a well-developed psychosis. He was incoherent in his speech, violent in his actions. I immediately noticed a well-defined arcus senilis on the pupil of the right eye—an arcus senilis, I may explain, is due to a hyaline, degeneration of the lamellae and cells of the cornea. It is, in my experience, indicative of the first stages of senile dementia.

"Disregarding, as I am afraid I must, because of the narrow latitude which is permitted me in my testimony, the history of the case and confining my testimony solely to what I myself saw, learned, and did when the patient had entered the hospital, I examined him for consciousness, orientation, hallucinations, delusions, idea association, memory, and judgment. I had already observed his unstable emotions."

"What did you find?" the lawyer asked.

"I found a case of well-defined senile dementia."

"And what is your suggestion in regard to this patient?"

"He should be placed under proper care and observation. With the passing of time, he will show a progressive mental deterioration and complete inability to handle his business affairs. He will become increasingly susceptible to blandishments, false friendships, and fraud. The progress of the disease can be stayed somewhat by proper care and treatment, relief from business worries, and particularly from the necessity of making decisions."

"And it was at your suggestion, Doctor, that the patient was not brought to court this morning?"

"Not only at my suggestion but because of my positive orders. In his present nervous state, the patient would become highly excited if he were brought into a public hearing. I would not care to be responsible for the results following such an appearance. Mr. Leeds is a very sick man mentally."

"You may cross-examine," the attorney said to Perry Mason.

Mason sat slumped down in the mahogany swivel chair at the counsel table, his long legs stretched out in front of him, his chin sunk on his chest. He did not look at the witness. "The patient was incoherent when you first saw him?" he asked, tonelessly.

"Yes."

"Excited?"

"Yes."

"Angry?"

"Yes."

"And from these things you diagnosed a senile dementia?"

"From those things and the other things."

"Well, let's take them up in order. These things helped to give you a diagnosis of senile dementia, did they not?"

"Yes."

"Anger and irritability are symptoms of senile dementia, Doctor?"

"Yes, sir, definitely."

"And I believe there is another similar disease, isn't there, Doctor, dementia praecox or schizophrenia?"

"That is not the same as senile dementia."

"So I understand, Doctor. In cases of dementia praecox, as I understand it, there is a condition of mental ataxia. The patient develops a state of apathy, becomes utterly indifferent to his surroundings, and cares nothing about what is done with him."

"That is right."

"Mr. Leeds was not suffering from that disease?"

"Certainly not. I have explained my diagnosis to you."

"If, on the other hand, you had noted any unnatural apathy of the emotions, you would have suspected dementia praecox?"

"I would have suspected it, yes."

"Well," Mason said moodily, still with his chin on his chest, "let's see where that leaves us, Doctor. A man, aged seventy-two years, goes out riding with his nephew. The nephew abruptly detours him to a sanitarium. Two male nurses come out of the sanitarium and start dragging him out of the car. You appear upon the scene. You find the patient angry and, as you have expressed it, incoherent. Wouldn't it be natural for a patient to be angry under such circumstances?"

"It depends on the circumstances."

"But if he *hadn't* been angry, you would have immediately diagnosed his condition as a lethargic symptom of mental ataxia, would you not?"

"I don't think that's a fair question."

"Perhaps not," Mason said, in the manner of one dismissing a subject. "Let's go on with your diagnosis. You found he was angry at being dragged out of the car. Therefore, you forthwith diagnosed his case as senile dementia, did you not?"

"I did not!" Dr. Londonberry exclaimed indignantly. "I have told you what factors entered into my diagnosis. Your question is a deliberate attempt to distort my testimony."

"Tut, tut," Mason said. "Don't work yourself up, Doctor. It wouldn't do for you to get angry—let's see, how old are *you*?"

"Fifty-six."

"A bit early for senile dementia to develop, is it not, Doctor?"

"Yes," the physician snapped.

"Then try and retain your good temper, Doctor, and I will try and be as fair as possible. You stated there were other symptoms. The only other symptom which you noted, I believe, was an arcus senilis."

"Well, that was sufficient."

"An arcus senilis, in your opinion, denotes a mental deterioration?"

"It is a symptom, yes."

"And just what is an arcus senilis, not in technical terms, but describe it."

"It appears as a crescent-shaped ring in the outer periphery of the cornea."

Mason suddenly raised his head. "Similar to the white crescent shape in the eye of His Honor, Judge Treadwell?" he asked.

Coincident with the asking of the question, Judge Treadwell leaned across the bench to stare at the witness.

Dr. Londonberry, startled, glanced up at the judge, then suddenly became confused. "Of course," he said, "an arcus senilis is not in itself indicative of psychosis. It is a symptom."

"Symptom of what?" Judge Treadwell asked acidly.

"A symptom of physical deterioration which, taken in connection with other symptoms, *may* indicate a mental deterioration."

"In other words," Judge Treadwell said, "if I should be taking a ride in an automobile, and two male nurses dragged me from the car, and I showed intense anger, that, coupled with my arcus senilis, would lead you to believe I was suffering from senile dementia, would it not?"

The witness fidgeted uneasily and said, "I hardly think that's a fair question, Your Honor."

"For your information," Judge Treadwell said, "I have had this arcus senilis for the last twenty-two years, and for your further information, I would be very much inclined to resent a highhanded interference with my liberties by any male nurses

31

at your institution, Doctor." He turned to Mason. "Are there any other questions, counselor?"

"None, Your Honor."

Judge Treadwell leaned forward. "The court thinks this examination has gone far enough. The court doesn't mind stating that this is merely another one of those cases in which a man, somewhat past the prime of life, is very apparently imposed upon by greedy and officious relatives, whose affection is predicated primarily on a financial consideration, and who are impatient that the object of their so-called affection is sufficiently inconsiderate to postpone shuffling the mortal coil, leaving behind, of course, a favorable will.

"Now the court is not in the least impressed with Dr. Londonberry's reason for not producing Alden Leeds in court. This court is getting more than a little out of patience with persons who feel that a judicial order is of no more importance than a tag for the violation of a parking ordinance. The court is going forthwith to Dr. Londonberry's sanitarium and examine the patient. If the court feels there is any necessity for doing so, the court will retain some reputable psychiatrist to pass upon the condition of Alden Leeds. If it appears that Alden Leeds is in the possession of his mental faculties to the extent usually found in a man of his years, the court is going to take drastic action for the flagrant and deliberate disregard of the court's order to produce the said Alden Leeds in court at this hour.

"Gentlemen, court will take a recess until two o'clock this afternoon. We will depart forthwith for Dr. Londonberry's sanitarium. The court will ask the bailiff to see that the sheriff's office furnishes transportation for Dr. Londonberry and the parties in the case. The court specifically warns anyone that any attempt to communicate with the sanitarium and prepare the persons in charge for the tour of inspection which is to be made will be considered as contempt of court."

"But, Your Honor," counsel shouted in protest. "This man is . . ."

"Sit down," Judge Treadwell said. "The court has made its order. Court is adjourned until two o'clock this afternoon."

The bailiff banged his gavel. Judge Treadwell marched with judicial dignity down the steps of the rostrum and through the door into chambers.

Some thirty minutes later, Mason parked his car in front of the sanitarium. The sheriff's car with Judge Treadwell, Freeman Leeds, Jason Carrel, Dr. Londonberry, and the attorney was waiting at the curb.

"Very well," Judge Treadwell said, "it appearing that the interested parties are here, we will now enter the sanitarium. Lead the way, Doctor, and please remember that we wish to drop in on the patient unannounced. I wish to see conditions as they are."

They entered the sanitarium.

Dr. Londonberry, as ruffled and indignant as a wet cat, led the way down a long corridor. A nurse, in a white, starched uniform came forward. "The key to thirty-five please," Dr. Londonberry said.

"You keep that door locked?" Judge Treadwell asked.

"Yes, we do," Dr. Londonberry said. "All he has to do is press a button when he wants anything. With patients of this sort, it's imperative to keep them quiet."

"Very well," Judge Treadwell said. "We'll see what the patient has to say for himself."

The nurse produced a key. Dr. Londonberry took it, fitted it to the lock in the door, flung it open, and stood to one side. "Some visitors for you, Mr. Leeds," he said. "I think you had better come first, Miss Leeds."

He bowed to Phyllis, then turned back, and stiffened in surprise.

There was no one in the room.

For several silent seconds, the little group stood there, staring at a cheerful room containing an immaculate hospital bed with snowy white linen, a reclining chair, a white enameled bedroom table, and a dresser with a mirror. A bathroom door, standing open, disclosed a white tile floor, a porcelain washstand with a medicine cabinet and mirror on the wall. Part of a bathtub was visible just beyond the open door.

Dr. Londonberry strode across the room, pushed open the bathroom door, looked inside, then turned swiftly on his heel, and, completely disregarding the group, pushed his way through them to stand in the corridor and summon the nurse. "Where's the patient in thirty-five?" he asked.

She stared at the room in surprise. "Why, he was there less than an hour ago."

Judge Treadwell crossed the room to stare at the window around which an ornamental, iron grille work shut off a little balcony some four feet wide.

Dr. Londonberry said, somewhat hastily, "That's a precaution we take with most of the rooms on the ground floor. It keeps the patient from escaping."

"It evidently didn't keep this one," Judge Treadwell said dryly.

"I beg your pardon," Dr. Londonberry observed, opening the window and shaking the iron grating. "The patient didn't leave by this window. . . . Where are his clothes, nurse?"

"In the locker room, locker thirty-five."

"Get them," Dr. Londonberry said.

Judge Treadwell observed almost tonelessly, "I take it, this patient isn't wandering around clad in a nightgown."

"He was wearing pajamas, a dressing gown, and slippers," Dr. Londonberry said.

He opened the bottom dresser drawer. It was empty save for some towels and clean sheets. He opened the second drawer, and disclosed a neatly folded dressing gown on top of which were pajamas and slippers.

"Good Heavens!" he said. "The man must be naked!"

They heard the patter of running steps in the corridor. The nurse returned to stare at them in white-faced consternation. "The locker door was closed and locked," she said. "The clothes are gone."

Phyllis Leeds exclaimed, "I don't believe it! This is some trick they've thought up."

"If it's a trick," Judge Treadwell said, "it will prove an expensive one for the parties who perpetrated it. I'll see that they
34

occupy a room where they'll be kept out of mischief for some time."

Dr. Londonberry said wrathfully to the nurse, "You're responsible for this. How could it have happened?"

"I'm sure I don't know, Doctor," she said, and her startled eyes and puzzled countenance indicated her complete mystification. "I looked in on the patient about an hour ago. About ten minutes later a man stopped me in the corridor, and said he was a visitor for Alden Leeds. I told him that orders were very strict, that Alden Leeds was to have no visitors. He said that . . ."

"This man stopped you in the *corridor*?" Dr. Londonberry interrupted. "How did he get in the *corridor*? Visitors are supposed to apply at the office."

"I don't know, Doctor," the nurse said. "He was here. That's all I know. I told him it would be absolutely impossible. He said the doctor in charge had told him it would be all right."

"The doctor in charge," Dr. Londonberry repeated.

"Yes, Doctor."

"Did he mention my name?"

"No, he just said the doctor in charge. He seemed quite positive about it, so I took him to the door of thirty-five, and showed him that there was a 'No Visitors' sign on it. I said that the patient was psychopathic, and under no circumstances were visitors permitted without direct orders from you. Shortly after that, the patient in fifteen had a sinking spell. That's a post-operative case, and I carried on the best I could. There was evidence of internal hemorrhage. I had my hands full until just a few moments ago when she rested easier. The last time I looked in here the patient seemed cheerful and quite relaxed."

"Can you describe this man who called as a visitor?" Judge Treadwell asked.

"He was wiry," the nurse said, "around fifty-five or sixty, I should judge, with gray eyes, and a weather-beaten face. He wore a tweed suit, and was smoking a pipe. He wore his hair rather long. It was brownish in color, faded somewhat, with streaks of gray at the temples, and . . ."

"Ned Barkler," Phyllis Leeds exclaimed, and then clapped her hand to her lips as though wishing to recall the words.

Judge Treadwell turned to her. "You know him?" he asked.

"One of Uncle's friends answers that description," Phyllis Leeds said.

"One who has been co-operating with the other relatives?" Judge Treadwell asked, significantly.

"No, Your Honor—Of course, I can't be sure that's the man, but the description fits.—He's an old prospecting pal of Uncle's."

"Where does he live?" Judge Treadwell asked.

"He's been living in the house with Uncle Alden."

Judge Treadwell's face relaxed slightly. "Evidently," he said, "the patient wasn't quite as incompetent as you thought, Doctor."

He turned to Phyllis Leeds and said, "I think you'll find that your uncle is now at home. I suggest that you go there at once— As for you, Doctor, I feel that your refusal to produce Alden Leeds in court was an act in defiance of the court's order. You will be ordered to appear and show cause why you should not be found guilty of contempt of court.

"I think that is all."

He nodded to Phyllis Leeds and said, "Simply for my own satisfaction, I'd be glad to know if you find your uncle at home. The deputy sheriff will drive you there at once."

Chapter 5

Perry Mason, with Della Street at his side, drove rapidly toward the city.

"What happened in the sanitarium?" Della asked. "Everyone came out in a hurry, and they hustled Phyllis Leeds off in the sheriff's car."

Mason sketched the highlights of what had taken place.

"What'll happen next?" Della Street asked.

"We'll go to the office," he said. "Phyllis Leeds will probably telephone us that her uncle is at home. The court will want him brought in when the *habeas corpus* hearing is re-opened. That'll be all there is to it."

"Where will that leave us?" Della asked.

"All finished," Mason said, "unless Leeds wants us to do something about that twenty thousand dollar check."

"Do you think he will?"

"No," Mason admitted, "I think he'll be sore we've done as much as we have.—And I can't get over my hunch that John Milicant is really L. C. Conway."

"Has Paul Drake found out anything?"

"I haven't been in touch with him for a while," Mason said. "He telephoned he had some routine stuff to report. I told him to let it wait until after the *habeas corpus*. I'll step on it and get back to the office in time to hear what he has to say before we go back to court."

"You're stepping on it now, Chief," she said, glancing at the speedometer.

Mason grinned. "You haven't seen anything yet. Look at *this*."

"I'm looking," she observed, "—and you missed that boulevard stop entirely."

"I didn't miss it," Mason said. "I took it in my stride."

"Stride is right. You . . ." She broke off as the low wail of a siren directly behind them signaled them over to the curb.

In stolid silence, Mason sat at the wheel while the officers pulled alongside. One of them, leaving the prowl car, started to make out a ticket. The other stood with an arrogant foot on the running board and bawled, "Where's the fire?"

"Central and Clark," Mason said.

The officer seemed taken aback. "What's burning?" he asked.

"My office."

"Say, are you kidding me, or on the square?"

"I don't know," Mason said. "All I know is what I heard on the telephone. My important papers are in danger. Naturally, I want to get there."

"Let's see your card, buddy."

Mason handed him a card. "Perry Mason, eh? Okay, let that ticket go, Jim. Let's take this guy up to his office. If it's a stall, we'll see that he gets the limit. You follow me."

The prowl car took the lead, siren screaming. Mason fell in behind.

"As I was observing," he said to Della, as they flashed through an intersection where traffic was frozen into inactivity by the screaming siren of the police car, "I take 'em in my stride."

"You'll get the limit for this," she warned.

"At any rate, we'll get to the office," he said.

"And waste time explaining to a lot of cops."

"No," Mason said, deftly dodging a truck, "you can't explain to these birds. This is one thing you *can't* explain."

"Chief, what *are* you going to do about it?"

"Darned if I know," he admitted, with a grin, "but it's a swell ride, isn't it, Della?"

"Listen, Chief, you can be as goofy as you want, but count *me* out."

38

He risked flashing her a swift glance. "Kidding?" he asked.

"No, I mean it."

"Getting chicken, Della?"

"You can call it that if you want," she said indignantly. "I'm going to get out."

"How? I can't stop now."

"No, but there'll be an opportunity. . . .Here, they're slowing down for that traffic jam. Chief, let me out!"

Mason slammed on the brakes. His profile was granite-hard. "Okay, baby," he said. "Write your own ticket."

"I'd rather do that than take the one the cops will write," she said, opening the door and jumping to the street just as the traffic jam ahead resolved itself, and Mason speeded up, following the siren of the police car.

They cut speed somewhat as they turned into the main artery. The officers ceased using the siren, worked their way through a traffic signal and parked in front of a reserved zone. Mason slid his car to a stop behind them.

"No sign of a fire here," one of the officers said belligerently.

"It's up in my office, I tell you, just a small fire. My God, you didn't think the *building* was afire, did you?"

The officers exchanged glances and sized Mason up. "Okay, Jim," the leader said, "you go up with this bird; I'll stay here. If this thing is a stall, pinch him for reckless driving. We can take him to headquarters on that. Perry Mason, attorney-at-law, eh?—Well, brother, you're like a lot of these wise guys. There's a little law you don't know."

Mason shrugged his shoulders. A boyish, carefree grin was on his face. "Wasn't that a swell ride?" he asked.

"Come on," the officer announced, grabbing Mason's elbow and half pushing him through the doorway and into the elevator.

Mason lit a nonchalant cigarette while the elevator deposited him at his floor. "Okay, buddy," the officer said, "you find the fire."

Mason strode down the corridor, jerked open the door to the entrance room of his office. A blast of pungent smoke met his nostrils. The girl who customarily occupied the information desk was dashing madly about with a cup of water. The stenographers were staring with startled eyes.

"Where's the fire?" Mason shouted at the girl with a water glass.

"In your private office," she said. "I think we got it in time."

Mason and the officer reached the private office. A wastebasket filled with charred papers was sending up wisps of smoke. A hole had been burnt in the carpet. The side of Mason's desk was scorched.

The girl from the switchboard, a tall, thin girl with spectacles, talked rapidly as Mason and the officer surveyed the damage. "I'm sorry," she said, "I didn't know what it was. You were on the telephone, and I screamed, when I saw the smoke, that the place was on fire. I don't know *how* those papers got started. One of the girls must have been in your private office and dropped ashes from her cigarette. It had a pretty good start before I found it, but it's all right now. How did you ever get here so quickly?"

Mason said, "I'll fire those girls. Find out which one did it, and give her her time. That's one thing I've particularly cautioned them against." He whirled to the officer, thrust out his hand, and said, "Thanks to you, Jim, old boy, we got here in time. The girls might not have been able to handle it. There are valuable papers in that desk, also some darn good cigars. How about taking a handful for you and your buddy?"

The officer was grinning. "Well, now," he said, "that's better. Who was it said, 'A woman is only a woman, but a good cigar is a smoke?'"

Mason, handing out a double handful of cigars, said, "No, Jim, I can't subscribe to those sentiments. Recent events have convinced me that women are vastly underrated."

The officer said, "Well, you may have something at that."

Mason escorted the officer to the corridor. "Say, what happened to the girl who was in the car with you?" the officer asked.

40

Mason laughed. "She couldn't stand the pace," he said. "Frightened her to death."

As the cage took the officer down, an ascending elevator paused to discharge Della Street. Mason looked at her and laughed. "Well," he said, "you fooled me."

Her voice showed nerve strain. "I had to. I wasn't certain I could put it across, so I didn't want to tell you about it. Did it work?"

"I'll say it worked! Incidentally, Gertrude gets a raise in pay."

"She needs it," Della Street said. "What are you doing out here in the corridor?"

"Just getting rid of the cops."

They walked down the corridor together. Mason latch-keyed the office door to find Gertrude down on hands and knees scrubbing at the charred carpet.

"Gertrude," he said, "arise and receive the benediction of the Order of Traffic Violators. You're a girl after my own heart. In the bottom right-hand drawer of that desk you'll find a bottle of whiskey and glasses. While you're pouring the whiskey, Della will make out the check which raises your salary twenty dollars a month, effective from the first of last month.—Were you frightened?"

She looked at him with emotions struggling into expression. "A twenty dollar raise!" she exclaimed.

Mason nodded.

She said, "Gee. . . Thanks, Mr. Mason. I. . . I. . ."

Mason gravely opened the desk drawer, took out a bottle of whiskey and glasses. Gertrude Lade, tall, thin as a rail, her figure angular, her face plain, took the glass of whiskey Mason handed her, grinned at them, and said, "Here's regards." She tossed off the whiskey in a single swallow, handed Mason back the empty glass, and said, "Listen, Mr. Mason, any time you want anything pulled around here, don't be afraid to call on me, and . . . thanks for that raise."

She turned and walked with long-legged strides through the door to the outer office.

41

Mason finished his whiskey, set down the empty glass, grinned at Della Street, and said, "She talks like a trouper."

"She sure does," Della Street said. "I was afraid I'd have to argue with her. I didn't. All I said was, 'The boss is in a jam. Go into his office and set fire to a wastebasket where it'll do about ten dollars' worth of damage." I waited for her to ask questions and argue. All she said was, 'Is that all?' "

Mason chuckled, picked up the telephone, and said, "Tell Paul Drake to come in, Gertrude." He hung up the telephone, looked at Della Street, and chuckled again. "Getting a girl for that information desk and switchboard has been something of a job," he said, "but I think we have one now. That remark of hers is priceless."

"Her voice didn't show the least excitement," Della Street said. "She was just as casual about it as though I'd told her to mail a letter."

Mason said, "Well, we'd better get this whiskey away before Drake comes in, or he'll mooch our booze as well as our cigarettes. Della, call Emily Milicant, and tell her I want to see her as soon as she can get here."

Della Street gathered up the empty glasses. "I'll wash these, and bring them back," she said.

A few seconds later, Drake knocked at the door, and Mason let him in.

Chapter 6

The detective draped himself over the black leather chair as limply lugubrious as crepe hanging on a door. "Hell," he said, "that bozo is as wise as a treeful of owls."

"Meaning Milicant?" Mason asked.

"Meaning Milicant," Drake said. "I put a man on him when he left your office, and got another man to tag along for relief. Milicant never even looked back. He went right along about his business, leading the fellows on a merry chase while he put on a swell act of a man about town keeping business appointments. Then when he got ready, he ditched them so neatly that it wasn't even funny. Of course, he made a beautiful build-up by never looking behind him, never acting at all suspicious, and going right on about his business."

"Any chance it was accidental?" Mason asked.

"None whatever," Drake said. "These boys weren't exactly amateurs, you know—even if Milicant did make them look like it."

"That makes him look more and more like Conway," Mason said.

"It does for a fact."

"All right, Paul," Mason said. "Within the next few minutes, Emily Milicant is going to be at the office. I'm going to tell her things which will make her hunt up her brother. You have men ready to take over when she leaves the office."

"Sounds like you're gunning for big game," Drake said.

"I'm going right on down the line, Paul. What else do you know, anything?"

Drake said, "I gathered you wanted me to look up Emily Milicant's past."

"Did I tell you to?" Mason asked.

"Not in so many words," Drake said. "I read your mind."

Mason said, "Nice going, Paul, only remember it was telepathy. What have you found out?"

"Not too much," Drake said. "I expect more details as soon as my Seattle agency runs down a couple of leads."

"Why Seattle?" Mason asked.

"She used to be a dance hall girl."

"In Seattle?"

"No, in the Klondike."

"When?" Mason asked.

"Around 1906 and 1907. Ever hear of the *'M and N Dance Hall'* in Dawson, Perry?"

"Seems to me I've heard something about it."

Drake said, "There were two dance halls, the *'M and N'* and the *'Flora Dora.'* Emily Milicant was in the *'M and N.'*"

Mason said, "Well, now we're commencing to get some place. That makes Emily Milicant a lot more understandable to me. She *may* have known Leeds up in the Klondike. Get your men working, Paul, and let's see what they can turn up."

"Okay," Drake said. "How did you burn the carpet, Perry?"

"Oh," Mason said, "Della did it.—It was arson. Get her to tell you about it sometime."

Drake jackknifed himself up out of the chair. "Hell, Perry, don't try to arouse *my* curiosity. I haven't any. I wouldn't investigate that damn carpet unless you paid me for it."

Mason grinned. "How about Emily Milicant?"

"She's different. How long do you want her tailed, Perry?"

"Only until she leads to Conway."

"Okay. I . . ."

The door from the outer office opened. Della Street came in with the three clean glasses. "Emily Milicant just came in," she said.

"Did you tell her you'd been trying to get her?" Mason asked.

"No."

"Good girl. What does she want?"

44

"Just to see if there's anything new."

Mason said, "Tell her I want to see her. Tell her to wait a minute."

Drake looked at the three whiskey glasses, and said significantly, "Guess I got here a little too late."

Mason took the glasses from Della Street, left them on the top of his desk. Drake grinned and said, "Oh, go ahead and put them in the drawer, Perry. I know where you keep it—the right-hand bottom drawer. I'd be a hell of a detective if I didn't know that."

Mason grinned. "Got some men you can put on Emily Milicant when she leaves, Paul?"

"Yes."

Mason said, "Any husbands in her life, Paul?"

"She's reputed to have married a man by the name of Hogarty," Drake said, "but I haven't the details."

"What happened to him? Was she divorced?"

"I don't know. I guess so. She's going under her maiden name."

The telephone rang. Mason said, "Wait a minute, Paul. This is probably Phyllis Leeds. I told Gertrude not to ring this phone unless it was someone connected with the Leeds case."

Mason said, "Hello," and Phyllis Leeds, talking rapidly, said, "Mr. Mason, Uncle Alden wasn't home. When we got here, the place had been ransacked."

"You mean the whole house?"

"No, Uncle Alden's study. Papers were all over the floor. Drawers were pulled out of the desks, and the filing cabinets were open. The sheriff went right to work on it.

"Listen, Mr. Mason. Uncle Alden gave another twenty thousand dollar check, payable to L. C. Conway and endorsed the same as the other one was. This time the check was cashed by a woman around forty-five with black eyes and high cheekbones. At the same time she presented the check, she gave the cashier a letter in Uncle Alden's handwriting stating that if there was any delay about cashing the check, he would take his account out of the bank."

"Did this woman leave a name?" Mason asked.

"No. She seemed to know her rights. She was very curt. She insisted on having the money in cash. The bank cashier says it was unmistakably Uncle Alden's handwriting. He's very much concerned about it. He was tempted to refuse payment, but the note frightened him."

Mason said, "I want to see that check."

"I've arranged for that," she said. "I've already given instructions to the bank, and a messenger will have it in your office within the next ten minutes."

"Good girl," Mason said into the telephone. "How are you feeling, worried?"

"No," she said. "I think Uncle Alden can take care of himself, now that he's free, but I'm mad."

"At whom?" Mason asked.

She laughed and said, "I don't know. Sometimes I think it's Uncle Alden."

Mason said, "All right. Take it easy. Your uncle will show up all right. When was that check dated?"

"Today. It was drawn from the checkbook he carries with him in his pocket. I feel certain he must have written it after he got out of the sanitarium."

Mason said, "Let me know if anything new turns up."

"What do *you* know, anything?" she asked.

"We're plugging along," Mason said.

"If you find Uncle, will you let me know?"

"Certainly. Do you want me to have Drake send out a woman operative to stay with you?"

"No," she said. "Why should I want anyone?"

"I thought you might be nervous, what with the study having been ransacked."

"I'm all right," she said, "but if I catch anyone prowling around the house, he's going to wish I hadn't. I'm mad enough to shoot someone."

"All right," Mason said. "Keep me posted. 'By."

He hung up and gave Paul Drake a digest of what Phyllis Leeds had told him.

Drake shook his head. "We're supposed to be working for Alden Leeds," he said. "I have a hunch we aren't actually helping him any."

"Perhaps not," Mason said.

"I think Leeds is going to be sore when he finds out about it."

"I think he knows about it," Mason said. "He's been in circulation for a while, and he seems to get around pretty fast, once he starts moving. He hasn't given any stop orders. Go to it, Paul. We'll get all the information we can. Tell your Seattle agency to show some speed."

"I've already told them," Drake said, "and I'll pick Emily up as she leaves the office. So long."

He ambled out through the outer door, moving as casually as though he had all the time in the world.

Mason said to Della Street, "Show Emily Milicant in. When the bank sends up the second check, Della, rush it over to our handwriting expert. Dig up some genuine samples of Leeds' handwriting."

Della Street nodded and quietly withdrew.

Mason opened his desk drawer and took out the pair of loaded dice. Drake had given him. He sat there, rolling them easily across the desk.

Emily Milicant was very much excited and showed it. Her eyes seemed unnaturally large and glittering. The hollows of her cheeks were more pronounced, the quick nervousness of her gestures more emphasized.

"Isn't it the most *horrible* thing?" she said. "I've been talking with Phyllis over the telephone."

Her eyes watched Mason's hand as he rolled the dice. The motion seemed to increase her nervousness.

"I'm anxious to know something about your brother," Mason said.

"My brother!" she echoed.

Mason nodded.

"I understand you asked Phyllis to bring him in, and asked him some questions about a crap game. Would you mind telling me what it's about?"

47

Mason said evenly, "What I'm particularly interested in is whether a shrewd lawyer could show that your brother regarded you as a means of support."

"What do you mean, Mr. Mason?"

Mason pounced upon the uneasy expression which crept into her eyes, as an alert cat jumps on a mouse. "Have you," he asked, "ever supported your brother?"

"Why . . . I hardly know how to answer that question."

"A lawyer," Mason observed, "would ask you to answer it 'yes' or 'no.'"

"Why, I suppose every sister helps out her brother from time to time. She'd be a poor sister if she didn't."

"Exactly," Mason agreed. "That brings us to the question of what you mean by 'from time to time.'"

"Why, whenever a man finds himself in a pinch, or when there's an emergency."

"Has your brother ever given anything to you for *your* support?" Mason asked.

"No, I was thrown out on the world when I was a child. I had to earn my own way."

"But you've helped out your brother?"

"Yes."

"Often?"

"Occasionally."

"In the form of loans?"

"I suppose so, yes."

"How much of those loans have been repaid?"

"Why . . . I don't know. . . . You don't consider your brother the same way you would a stranger. I . . . I don't keep any account of it."

"How much money have you given him in all?"

"I don't know. I tell you I never kept track of it."

"As much as a thousand dollars?"

"I guess so, yes."

"Two thousand?"

"Perhaps."

"Three?"

"Really, Mr. Mason, I don't see the object of this."

"Four?"

"But, Mr. Mason . . ."

"Five?"

She straightened indignantly, and said, "What difference does it make?"

Mason said, "If he goes on the witness stand, a judge is quite apt to rule that it's proper cross-examination as showing the extent of his interest. Was it as much as six?"

Her eyes, blinking rapidly, showed indignation. "It may have been."

"As much as ten?"

"I don't know."

"Of this amount," Mason asked, "has he ever repaid a dime?"

"I couldn't tell you."

Mason gently shook the dice together in his cupped hands. She watched him as if fascinated. He rolled them out with a long, sweeping gesture.

"For Heaven's sake!" she snapped out. "Stop rolling those dice!"

"What's the matter?" Perry asked, putting the dice down on the desk. "Don't you like the bones?"

"No—. Yes," she said. "Oh, I don't know, you just make me nervous."

Mason said, "Now, let me ask you another question. Did you ever hear of the Conway Appliance Company?"

"The name is familiar. Oh, I know. That was the name on the check. Alden gave the check to L. C. Conway."

"That's right," Mason said. "The company specializes in the sale of crooked crap dice—like this pair—and includes, as a 'premium,' a lottery ticket. The company was originally operated by L. C. Conway. Then, a few days ago, it was apparently sold to a man named Serle—Guy T. Serle, who has moved the business to 209 East Ranchester Avenue. Does any of that mean anything to you?"

"Not a thing."

Mason said, "Look here, Miss Milicant, I'm going to be frank with you. Here's a description of L. C. Conway— approximately fifty-five, five feet ten inches, weight around one hundred and eighty, heavy features, partially bald with black hair coming to a peak near the center of his head. Has a slight limp. Does that description mean anything to you?"

She met his eyes. "Is it supposed to?"

"I thought it might."

"The description," she said abruptly, "fits my brother," and Mason noticed that her hands were gripping the arms of the chair.

Mason said, "So it does," as though the idea had just occurred to him. "Are you trying to suggest to me that your brother and L. C. Conway are one and the same?"

She said, "I thought *you* were the one who was trying to suggest that to *me*."

Mason said, "I think you'd better check up on your brother and the possibility that he is the L. C. Conway who got that twenty thousand dollar check from Alden Leeds."

Her face was white enough so that the patches of orange rouge ceased to blend with her natural color. "He couldn't have done that," she said slowly, "simply *couldn't*—not after all I've done for him. It would be a terrible, a wicked thing to do."

Mason said carelessly, "I believe Leeds made the bulk of his fortune from a gold strike up in the Yukon, did he not?"

"I've heard him say something like that."

"Must be a great country," Mason said.

"That was years ago," she pointed out.

"Ever been up there?" the lawyer inquired.

She met his eyes steadily, and said, "No."

"How about John?" Mason inquired. "I wonder if he was ever up in the Klondike or the Yukon?"

Again she met his eyes, and again, in the same positive voice, said, "No."

Mason smiled to signify that the interview was over. "Thanks a lot," he said.

For the moment, she made no move to leave. "Could you . . .

would you . . . tell me just how it was you happened to suspect John of being L. C. Conway?"

Mason's smile was both affable and evasive. "I thought," he said, "the suggestion came from you. I read you Conway's description, that was all."

She recognized the note of dismissal in his voice and came to her feet. "Does Phyllis know anything about this?" she asked.

"No one knows, outside of my office staff and those who are working with me."

Ten minutes after Emily Milicant had left, Della Street announced that Ned Barkler was in the office.

Mason told her to bring him in, and, a few seconds later, was shaking hands with the calmly competent, completely unperturbed prospector.

"Hello," Barkler said, his pipe clamped between his teeth. "Ain't seen Phyllis, have you?"

"No," Mason said. "I think she's out at the house."

"Nope. She ain't there."

"Perhaps she went to the bank. Were you out at the house?"

Barkler sat down, pushed the tobacco down into the bowl of his pipe with a horny forefinger, and said, "Some cops were out at the house messing around with fingerprints and stuff. They tried to shake me down, and I told them where they got off."

"Alden Leeds' study was ransacked," Mason said.

"Uh huh," Barkler agreed.

Mason, eyeing the man curiously, said, "How did you happen to locate Alden Leeds?"

"Where?"

"At the sanitarium."

A network of little wrinkles appeared around Barkler's amused eyes. He took the pipe from his mouth to chuckle softly. Mason, sizing up his man, made no effort to crowd him, but tilting back in his swivel chair, lit another cigarette and waited.

After a few moments, Barkler went on, "That crowd sure must'a thought Alden was getting simple. Christ A'mighty, Alden's been through things those stay-at-home bastards never even dreamt of—and taken them all in his stride. Why, he was in a mutiny one time . . . well, no . . . I guess he wasn't either."

"Leeds got in touch with you?" Mason prompted.

"Uh huh, there was a couple of heavy rubber bands holding the curtains together in the bathroom. Alden slipped them off, tied them together, and then tied the ends to the iron bars on the window. He wrote a note asking whoever found it to ring me up and tell me where he was. Then he wrapped a little piece of soap in the paper to give it weight. . . ." Barkler broke off to chuckle. His chuckling started a fit of coughing. His pipe went out, and he scratched a match to light it again.

"It worked?" Mason asked.

"Worked!" Barkler said. "I'll say it worked. . . . Heh, heh, heh. . . . A guy walked past out in the street, and Alden turned loose his slingshot, and darned if he didn't hit the guy right in the leg. The guy was sore for a minute, but he looked up and seen Alden in the window of the sanitarium. Alden made signs to him, so he picked up the note and read it and waved his hand to show that he understood. Guess he thought Alden was a nut all right, but he figured it wouldn't do no harm to let me know where he was."

Mason said, "Didn't you know that Phyllis was bringing the matter up in court?"

Barkler's laugh was like the sound of a wind rustling dry leaves. "What the hell does Alden and me want with court?" he asked. "Courts be damned! I strapped on the old persuader, and went down to get him out—figured I might have to get rough. But shucks, they was dead simple. I could have stole them blind."

Mason grinned. "You knew Leeds up in the Klondike, didn't you?"

"Tanana," Barkler corrected.

"All the same, isn't it?" Mason asked.

"Nope," Barkler said shortly.

"Must have been a wild country," Mason ventured.

"It was. A man that couldn't take care of himself had no business being up in that country."

"Were you around Dawson?" Mason inquired.

"Yep, all through that country."

"They had some wild dance halls in Dawson, didn't they?"

"Depends on what you call wild. A man could get lots of action. I've seen wilder places."

"Know any of the dance hall girls?" Mason inquired.

"Some."

"Ever know Emily Milicant before she showed up here?" Mason asked.

Barkler didn't answer the question for several seconds. He puffed at his pipe, his keen, frosty eyes regarding Mason through the white smoke. "I'm checking out," he said.

"Why?" Mason asked. "What's the matter?"

"Nothing's the matter. I'm just checking out. I don't like cops—a bunch of damn busybodies, if you ask me, messing around and wanting to take a guy's fingerprints."

"Did they want yours?"

"Yep."

"Get them?"

"Nope."

"Where," Mason asked, "is Alden Leeds now?"

"Out attending to some business."

"Do you know where he is?"

"He'll show up when he gets ready."

Mason said, "I'm very anxious to see him. It's important."

"Uh huh."

"If you see him or if you can get a message to him, will you let me know?"

"Nope."

"You won't?"

"Nope. Alden can get in touch with you if he wants to. He wanted me to come in and give you a message."

"What," Mason asked, "was the message?"

"He wanted me to tell you that he was all right, and not to worry about him, but to keep right on working just the way you're doing now."

Mason said, "He seems to keep pretty well posted."

Again Barkler chuckled. "He does," he said. "Alden's no-body's fool. Well, let's see now. . . . Oh, yes, he said to tell you to stall around and get as much time as you could, and to tell Phyllis not to worry."

"He isn't going back to his house?" Mason asked.

"Not right away, I don't think," Barkler said.

"Why?"

"You'll have to ask Alden about that."

"If I don't know where he is, I can't ask him," Mason said, with a smile.

"That's right," Barkler agreed seriously. "You can't."

He got to his feet, crossed over to the cuspidor, tapped ashes out of his pipe, and said, "Well, I'll be getting on. Tell Miss Phyllis I'm checking out for a while."

"You mean you won't be back for several days?"

Barkler said, "Uh huh," and walked across to the exit door.

Mason said, "Just a minute, Barkler, before you leave. If I'm not going to see Alden Leeds, there are some papers which he'll have to sign. They're in the outer office. Wait here a minute, and I'll get them for you."

Mason strode quickly to the door leading to the outer office. Barkler said, "Don't be long," walked back to the leather chair, and sat down.

Gertrude Lade looked up from the telephone desk as Mason approached. "Where's Della?" he asked.

"Went out with some papers to a handwriting expert."

Mason said, "Beat it down to Paul Drake's office. Tell him Ned Barkler is in my office, that he's leaving right away; to put a tail on him. Hurry."

Gertrude Lade paused only to ask one question. "Does Mr. Drake know him, or do I describe him?"

"Drake knows him," Mason said.

She jerked off the headset and started for the door on the run. Mason paused only long enough to take the Leeds file from the filing case, then walked back to his private office. As he opened the door, he said, "I want you to tell me if . . ." and broke off into

54

surprised silence as he realized the office was empty. He jerked open the exit door and sprinted down the corridor to the elevator. The corridor was deserted.

Chapter 7

It was after midnight when Perry Mason and Della Street, flushed and laughing, entered Paul Drake's office. The man who was on duty at the switchboard knew Perry Mason.

"The boss in?" Mason asked.

"Yes. Just go in. I'll tell him you're coming."

They walked along the reception hallway, pushed open a swinging door at the end, entered a filing room, and beyond that, pushed open the door to an eight-by-ten office where Drake had contrived to place a small desk, a swivel chair, three telephones, a filing case, and a steel safe.

Mason said, "I know now why you like to sprawl all over our office, Paul. There isn't room for you to unlax here. You have to sit straight as a ramrod to keep your feet from slipping out of the office during the middle of a conference."

Drake, violently chewing gum, consulted the three memo pads, one in front of each telephone, and said, "Give Della the chair over there, Perry. You can sit on the corner of the desk. What sort of a run-around were you giving me with this Barkler guy?"

Mason laughed. "Guess I was a little crude there, Paul. I tipped my hand."

One of the telephones rang. Drake, chewing his gum violently, scooped the receiver to his ear, said, "Hello. Yes—okay, give it to me," and started making notes. In the midst of the notetaking, the other telephone rang. Drake picked it up, said into the transmitter, "Hold the line for just a minute," finished making notes, said, "Okay, Frank. Hang on for a minute. Something's coming in over the other telephone." He said, "All right," into the second transmitter and translated the metallic sounds which came through the receiver into notes on the pad in front of him, said, "Report again in an hour," and hung up. He said into the first telephone, "Okay, keep the place sewed up. Don't let him get away. Make a report as soon as he does anything."

"I take it," Mason said, "you've struck pay dirt."

Drake spat his chew of gum into a wastebasket, opened a drawer, took out two fresh sticks, fed them rapidly into his mouth.

"He gets this way when things get hot," Mason explained to Della Street.

Della, watching the detective's jaw with fascination said, "If there were only some way of harnessing that motion to a dynamo, we could run the elevator in the building."

Drake grinned at her, and said, "Go ahead, folks, have your fun. I can see you've been painting the town red while I've been holding my nose to a grindstone."

"My God!" Mason exclaimed. "Don't tell me there's a grindstone in here, too!"

Drake pulled the nearest memo pad over toward him. "Want the report?" he asked.

"I suppose we've got to have it," Mason said.

Drake said, "I have an idea we let the biggest game slip through our fingers, Perry. It couldn't have been helped, but I'm kicking myself just the same."

"How so?" Mason asked.

Drake said, "Emily Milicant left your office, but didn't go to her apartment. She kept calling a number from public phones and getting no answer. The fourth time she tried, one of my men got close enough to watch the number she was dialing. It was Westhaven one-two-eight-nine. I looked it up, and found that it was an unlisted number, in the name of L. C. Conway at apartment 625 in an apartment house at 513 Haldemore Avenue.

"I immediately sent a man down to cover that apartment, and we continued camping on Emily Milicant's trail."

"Good work, Paul," the lawyer said.

Drake paused long enough to shift his gum from one side to the other and work it into place with half a dozen nervously rapid chews.

"Okay," he said, "here's what happens. Around six o'clock Emily Milicant goes down to that apartment house. She went up in the elevator around six o'clock and was out about six-five. She'd led us to Conway, so we dropped her, and I put operatives in the lobby to check everyone who took the elevators to the sixth floor. There's a floor register over the elevator.

"At six-twenty-nine, John Milicant comes in. He's accompanied by a tall, thin chap around forty that my operative identifies as Guy T. Serle. You remember he's the one who took over the Conway Appliance Company. They're smoking cigars. Serle seems sore as hell about something. After we got the dope later on, we found out how he could be sore."

"What was the dope?" Mason asked.

"Police raided the Conway Appliance Company about five o'clock this afternoon. They confiscated a lot of equipment, picked up a couple of underlings, and there's a felony warrant out for Serle."

"Think he knew it when he was with Milicant?" Mason asked.

"He acted like it."

"Okay," Mason said, "go on."

"Well, Serle went in at six-twenty-nine and out at six-thirty-eight. At six-fifty-seven, a blonde baby, who impressed the operative on duty as being a million dollars' worth of pulchritude, went in, and five minutes later came out. From the description, I figure she's Marcia Whittaker, although the operative didn't know Marcia Whittaker.

"At seven-forty-one, Serle comes in again. At eight-ten, a restaurant a couple of doors down the street sent up two dinners. The operative checked back and found that the order had been telephoned in to the restaurant right around five minutes to eight. Evidently, Serle and Conway had a little more stuff to talk over, and grabbed a quick dinner while they were doing it."

"Why quick?" Mason asked.

58

"Because Serle was out again at eight-twenty-three. A waiter called for the dishes at ten-forty. Well, now, here's where we pulled our boner. At ten-five a man went in who was a stranger to all the operatives. He was an oldish man, thin, white haired, and straight as a ramrod. He was dressed in blue serge, didn't wear an overcoat, had black patent leather shoes, and was smoking a cigar."

"How long did he stay?" Mason asked.

"Eleven minutes. He was out at ten-sixteen."

"How did you pull a boner, Paul?"

Drake said, "Because I figure this guy was Alden Leeds."

"You didn't tell Phyllis Leeds that, did you?" Mason asked apprehensively.

"Hell, no," Drake said. "It's bad enough to pull a boner, without telling a client about it."

Mason nodded thoughtfully. Della Street said, "I don't see how you could have done things any differently, Paul."

"I couldn't," Drake admitted, "unless I'd been up on my toes and played a hunch. You see reports were relayed to me. By the time I got this guy's description, he'd left. But good detective work consists of a lot of luck and a lot of hunch playing. I might have anticipated Leeds would drop in, and been ready for him. I muffed that play.

"Well, that's practically all. At ten-twenty-one, the blonde girl came back again. This time she was carrying an overnight bag. It looked as though she'd dropped in, fixed things up with Milicant, and was back for a longer visit after Milicant had got rid of all the business."

"How long did she stay?" Mason asked.

"That's just it," Drake said. "She went in, and then came right back out at ten-thirty-two."

"Did she leave the bag?"

"No, she evidently hadn't even taken her hat off, just popped in and popped out again. I have a hunch something had happened, and Milicant wasn't as glad to see her as she thought he was going to be."

"Meaning what?" Mason asked.

"Meaning the sister," Drake said. "The girl was in first at six-fifty-seven and was out by two minutes past seven. She came out looking happy. The next time the blonde shows up, the situation is radically different, and she comes out with her shoulders squared, her chin up in the air, and walks to the corner where she grabs a taxi."

"Anything happen after that?" Mason asked.

"Not a thing," Drake said.

Mason said, "Hell, Paul, I don't see how you do any business in this office. You can't pace the floor."

Drake started to say something when one of the telephones rang. He answered it, received evidently a routine report because he looked at his watch, made a note, said, "Okay, stay on the job and keep reporting," and hung up. Before he could turn to say anything to the lawyer, another phone rang, and Drake picked up the receiver, said, "Okay, this is Drake talking. Put them on." He turned to Mason, and said, "Seattle calling." A few moments later he said, "Yes, this is Paul Drake. Go ahead and tell me what you've found." Then for five minutes, beyond an occasional "Yes . . . Okay . . . Go on from there," he said nothing, but scribbled notes on a sheet of paper. He said, "Make a complete report by way of confirmation and send it on by airmail," hung up, and turned to Mason again. "That was my Seattle correspondent," he said. "They dug up old passenger lists of the steamship lines. Records show that Alden Leeds sailed for Dawson City via Skagway in 1906. In the latter part of 1906, he was reported in partnership with a man named Bill Hogarty in the Tanana country. Next winter it was reported Leeds was killed in a snowslide."

"Killed!" Mason exclaimed.

"That's the way the report runs. Shortly after that, Bill Hogarty came out. He'd struck it rich. Hogarty got as far as Seattle and vanished. Our correspondent wants to know if he's to try and pick up the Hogarty trail."

"Go to it, Paul," Mason said. "Start from there."

"Where do I stop?" Drake asked.

"Don't stop," Mason said. "Keep going," then, turning to Della Street, "Come on, Della. Let's go to an office where we can pace the floor."

"Going to be there for a while?" Drake asked.

"Probably not," Mason said. "With you on the job, I don't see why *we* should lose a lot of sleep."

Back in his office, Mason paced the floor, puffing away at his cigarette, his thumbs hooked in the armholes of his vest, his chin lowered, eyes fixed moodily on the carpet. All of the playboy spontaneity which had characterized him throughout the evening with Della Street had vanished.

Della Street sat in the big leather chair, her heels pulled up, her arms clasping her knees and holding her skirts tightly against her legs. Her eyes followed Perry Mason with solicitous concern.

The telephone sounded startlingly loud against the midnight silence of the office building.

"It must be Paul Drake," Della Street said.

"No, Paul Drake would come in here—unless something important has happened, and he doesn't dare to leave his own telephone."

He scooped up the receiver and said, "Hello."

A feminine voice said, "Mr. Perry Mason, the attorney?"

"Yes speaking. Who is this talking?"

"Long distance. San Francisco is calling you."

Mason frowned at the telephone and said, "And how did you know that my office hours were from six P.M. until two A.M.?"

The long distance operator ignored the sally. Her voice was crisp and businesslike. "I tried your apartment, Mr. Mason, and then called the office. Just a moment, please. . . . Go ahead. We're ready with your call to Mr. Mason."

A woman's voice, sounding thin and frightened, said, "Mr. Mason, this is Miss Whittaker. Do you remember me, Marcia Whittaker?"

"Certainly," Mason said. "Where are you now?"

"San Francisco."

"How did you get there? You were here around ten o'clock, weren't you?"

"Yes. I came up on a late plane. I'm calling from the airport now."

"All right," Mason said, "what is it?"

Her voice showed traces of hysteria. "I can't do it," she sobbed. "I can't run away from it. I thought I could, but I can't."

"Run away from what?" Mason asked.

"From what happened."

Her voice became almost a whisper. "I can't tell you—over the phone," she said.

Mason said, "Now listen carefully, Marcia, watch your answers. Does anyone know you're in San Francisco?"

"No."

"Have you quarreled with your boy friend?"

"No . . . not a quarrel. . . . I can't . . ."

"Is he angry?"

"No, no! Can't you understand? He isn't . . ."

"And he won't be angry?" Mason interrupted. "*Never* be angry again?"

"That's—that's right."

"We're representing Alden Leeds, you know," Mason said.

"Yes, I know. That's why I'm calling you. I have . . . have something for you . . . and you can help me."

"But only if it helps Leeds."

"I understand."

"This thing you have—is it important?"

"Very."

Mason thought rapidly. "You went to his apartment around ten-thirty tonight?"

"Yes. How did you know?"

Mason said, "Never mind that. Can you get a plane back?"

"Yes."

"Is there any way I can get a key to your apartment?"

"Yes, I keep my mailbox unlocked and there's an extra key in the bottom of the mailbox."

Mason said, "Get back here just as quickly as you can. Is there a telephone in your flat?"

"Yes."

"What's the number?"

"Graymore six-nine-four-seven."

"All right," Mason said. "Don't tell anyone about this conversation with me, do you understand?"

"Yes."

"Be seeing you," Mason said, and hung up.

He turned to Della Street. "You probably got most of it," he said, "from what I said at this end. Marcia Whittaker. It's an even money bet that John Milicant has either committed suicide or been murdered. I'm inclined right now to the suicide angle."

Della Street, with calm competence, took a notebook from her purse. "I took down the schedule as Paul Drake read it off," she said. "Do you want to know the people who came in during the evening?"

"No," Mason said, "they're not important. Serle had dinner with him. A man who answers the description of Alden Leeds was in at ten-five. The girl was there at ten-twenty-one. The man left just before the girl came. That's the picture. Whatever happened, happened late.

"These people stayed too long to have been standing in front of the door, knocking and waiting for an answer. It's hardly likely that both Leeds and Marcia would have stumbled on a dead body and said nothing about it. . . . Come on, Della, we're going to see Paul Drake."

They trooped back to Drake's office. Drake was just struggling into his overcoat.

"You again!" he said. "Why don't you go on out and make whoopee?—In other words, why don't you get the hell out of here and let working men get a decent night's sleep?"

Mason said, "Listen, Paul. You're not going home."

"That's what *you* think," Drake said. "It's after one."

Mason shook his head. "You're going right back and sit at that desk," he said. "You're going to keep on the telephone, in direct communication with your men who are watching

63

Conway's apartment. If there's anything unusual, any sign of activity, you're to telephone me at Graymore six-nine-four-seven. You're to memorize that number and not leave it hanging around on any slips of paper, and you're to forget this whole business tomorrow morning at ten o'clock."

Drake frowned. "What's the matter, Perry?" he asked.

Mason said, "Those are instructions, Paul. That's all you need to know. You won't want to know any more."

"Do I wait here all night?"

"All night or until we telephone you."

Drake slipped out of his overcoat, said to the man behind the arch-shaped window, "Go down to the all-night drugstore and get me four bits' worth of chewing gum."

Mason nodded to Della Street. "Come on, Della. We go within about three blocks of the place and walk the rest of the way."

Twenty minutes later, Mason's groping fingers encountered a key in the bottom of the mailbox marked "Marcia Whittaker." He latchkeyed the front door, switched on the stair lights, and noiselessly climbed the carpeted treads.

"Just what I was afraid of," Mason growled as he switched on lights in the flat and entered the bedroom.

Everywhere were evidences of hurried flight. The imprints of a suitcase showed on the white counterpane of the bed. Clothes had been laid out and discarded. Drawers had been opened and ransacked.

Mason glanced at Della Street. "How about it, Della," he asked, "can you put this place in order?"

"So the police won't know she packed to skip out?"

"Yes."

"Isn't that suppressing evidence, Chief?"

He said, "You're acting under my instructions. If anything goes wrong. I take the rap."

"Nothing doing," she said, slipping out of her coat. "We're in it together. Go out in the other room and sit down. Let me have a free hand here."

"Okay," Mason said. "Remember to keep your gloves on."

Thirty minutes later she joined him in the outer room. They sat together by the little fireplace talking in low tones and waiting for the phone to ring. Perry Mason's hand unconsciously sought Della Street's, gently imprisoned the fingers. "Gosh, Della," he said, "I'm getting sentimental. It almost seems as though this place had been made for *us*."

She moved her other hand to gently stroke the back of his well-shaped, strong fingers. "Nix on it, Chief," she said softly. "You could no more live a domestic life than you could fly. You're a free-lance, happy-go-lucky, carefree, two-fisted fighter. You might like a home for about two weeks, and then it would bore you stiff. At the end of four months, you'd feel it was a prison."

"Well," Mason said, "this is part of the first two weeks."

It seemed but a few minutes before they heard the click of a key in the lock. Mason glanced at his wrist watch. It was four-forty-five. Della Street, with a quick intake of breath, said, "I don't want her to see me until I powder my nose," and dashed for the bathroom.

The door slowly swung back. Marcia Whittaker, looking as though she'd been seeing a steady procession of ghosts, came wearily into the room, lugging a Gladstone bag.

She dropped the bag to the floor, came across the room, and held his arms with quivering fingers. "It's so darn square of you!" she said.

Mason patted her shoulder. "Nix," he said. "Get that bag unpacked."

Della Street came out of the bathroom, smiling a cordial welcome.

"My secretary," Mason said. "Della Street, Marcia Whittaker. Give her a hand, Della, if you will please."

Mason returned to sit by the fireplace smoking in thoughtful silence until Marcia and Della returned.

"All right," Mason said, "let's have it. I want exact, detailed information. You can't afford to indulge your emotions. Get right down to bedrock. You've cried before. You can cry afterward. Right now, you *can't cry*."

65

She said, "I can take it now, Mr. Mason. It was a hell of a wallop. I should have expected it. Life's done that to me ever since I was a kid."

"Forget that," Mason said. "I want facts—all the facts—and I want them fast."

She said, "I didn't give you a fair break the first time I saw you. I knew Louie Conway and John Milicant were the same. John's sister is a hypocrite. She's knocked around plenty in her time, but now she's developed complexes and wants the family to amount to something. I'm a little tart, and I mustn't be in the family—Oh, dear no!"

"Skip all that," Mason said. "Let's get down to brass tacks. What happened to Louie? Tell me . . ."

She stopped him with a gesture. "You have to know about this other," she said. "Let me tell it first—then I'll tell . . . tell the other."

"Go on," Mason said.

"Louie—John, is—was a good scout. He was too weak. I'm no tin angel myself. John liked good clothes, good cars. He hadn't the training for a job. He couldn't have held one down anyway. He went in for promoting. He liked horses, cards, dice, and gambling. . . . John wasn't young any more. Things were getting harder for him.

"I could understand him. His sister was figuring on marrying into a rich family. She wanted to keep the family background on the up and up, and make a nice impression on Alden Leeds. She had some dough, some settlement she got from a former husband. I don't know how much. She told John he'd have to become respectable—no ponies, gambling, or promoting—until she'd got her hooks into Alden Leeds.

"John wasn't the kind who could do that. His sister put him on an allowance. He stayed straight for a week or two, and then went back to the old life, keeping his sister in the dark. He took the name of Louie Conway and started the Conway Appliance Company. That was where I met him. I was clerking at a cigar counter. John came in and shook me a couple of games of twenty-six. He was lucky with dice all right, and the game was on the square. I've knocked around a bit myself, and I saw to that. A couple of customers came in and pretty quick they were shooting craps.

"John was rolling the dice. I was selling cigars. I saw the dice were crooked, but I didn't say anything. If the suckers wanted to get trimmed, that was up to them. The way I figure it, a sucker is a sucker. If John hadn't taken them, someone else would.

"Well, John knew that I'd spotted the dice. He came back later, and said, 'Sister, you've got a nice mouth.' I said, 'Most men talk about my eyes.' He said, 'I'm talking about your mouth. It stays closed at the right time. Here's fifty bucks. Buy yourself some glad rags.'

"I took a shine to him. I knew him as Louie Conway. We played around for a while. I was tired of living in little bedrooms and cheap furnished apartments with the furniture all battered up, and the thin mattresses having a ridge down the center.

"Louie got serious—and told his sister. She blew up, said everything was fixed with Alden Leeds and that it would ruin the play to have John bring a cigar-counter girl into the family.

"John wouldn't give me up. He pretended to his sister that he had. She was suspicious. John started scheming, and then, one day, he came to me and said he'd used the Conway connection to get a stake out of Alden Leeds, and Leeds would never know that Conway and John Milicant were one and the same person. He told me I'd have to help him put it across, that then we'd get married, and he'd tell his sister to go jump in the lake."

"Did you know what the shakedown was?"

"No, not then. I still don't know."

"Go on," Mason told her.

"I didn't want to do it. I'd never had a police record. I knew him well enough to know he was keeping himself in the background and pushing me out in front."

"You can skip that," Mason said. "Hell, we don't need a blueprint. You did it. Then what?"

"Of course, I did it!" she blazed. "And why not? And don't blame Louie too much either. Leeds is lousy with the dough. He

67

can't take it with him. It's all right to talk about respectability if you've been educated so you can get by and *be* respectable, but when you have nothing back of you, you have to take things as they come.

"That's the way John found life, and that's the way I found it. I suppose some women think I'm cheap and flashy, but . . . well, John thought I was swell, and I thought he was swell. . . . Anyhow, I was to go to his apartment at ten-thirty, and in the morning we were to get married, and be on our way. And . . . and I went up there about ten-twenty. I had a key. I walked on in, calling to John. I didn't get any answer. I looked around the place. Things had been turned topsy-turvy. I was frightened and I ran into the bathroom. John was in there on the floor with the handle of a carving knife st-st-sticking . . . sticking . . ." She broke into tears, shook her head, and dropped down into a chair. "I c-c-can't do it," she said. "I c-c-can't."

"Take it easy, Marcia," Mason told her. "I know how you feel, but you're loaded with dynamite. If you found John had been murdered and didn't notify the police, you're in a fix, and, now that you've told us, if *we* don't notify the police, we're in a fix. You're not our client. Alden Leeds is our client. This isn't a privileged communication. We're going off the deep end for you."

Marcia Whittaker took a quivering breath, and said, "I go nuts every time I think of it. . . . I knew what they were searching for. They didn't find it."

"How do you know they didn't find it?" Mason asked.

"Because I have it," she said.

Mason's eyes narrowed.

"Louie wasn't a fool," she said. "He knew that his apartment might be searched. He had to have this stuff where he could get at it at any time. He left it with me."

"What?"

"Papers."

"What kind of papers? What would they buy?"

"I don't know," she said. "I know that it got Louie twenty

grand, and he said it was going to get him another twenty grand, maybe another eighty grand, before he'd let go of them."

Mason, frowning thoughtfully, said, "Where did John get these papers?"

"I don't know," she said.

Mason said, "All right, Marcia. Where is the stuff?"

"I have it."

"Get it."

"If I do, what do I get?"

Mason said, "Are you holding an auction?"

She said, "Don't think *I'm* going to take the rap on this. Alden Leeds has dough. He can see me through. He's the only one who can."

"What's the proposition?" Mason asked.

"I give Alden Leeds the papers if he agrees to stand by me."

Mason thought for a moment, then said, "Suppose it should appear that Alden Leeds was in that apartment just before you were?"

She thought that over silently, then shook her head, and said, "No."

"I think he was," Mason said. "That puts you both on a spot. The natural way for you to get out is to try to pin the murder on him. The natural way for him to get out is to try to pin it on you."

"If he does that," she threatened, "I'll . . . I'll . . ."

"What?" Mason asked.

"I'm not exactly a fool," she said, after a moment.

"That trip to San Francisco sounds like it," Mason said.

"I came back, didn't I?"

Mason said, "Don't forget, Marcia, we're acting as Leeds' lawyers. We're cold-blooded about it."

"I know," she told him, "but I can trust you."

"What are these papers?" Mason asked.

"Mostly photographs," she said.

"Photographs of what?" Mason asked.

"Of old saloons, of a dance hall in Dawson City, of hotel registers, and a photostatic copy of a marriage license."

"Who got married?" Mason asked.

69

"Emily Milicant and a Bill Hogarty."

"Who signed the hotel registers?"

"Bill Hogarty."

Glancing across at Della Street, Mason said, "They may not be worth much."

"Louie got twenty grand as a starter, and there was more to follow."

"All right," Mason said. "Give me the papers."

She got up from the chair, and walked into the bedroom. They heard the door close, and a lock click. Della Street exchanged glances with Perry Mason.

Mason said, "There's something Alden Leeds wanted to cover up. The documents were only the blackmailer's card of introduction."

"How do you figure that, Chief?"

"Because Leeds paid twenty thousand, and *didn't get possession of the documents.*"

"Where does that put us, Chief?" she asked.

"Right on the end of the limb," Mason said.

The bedroom door opened. Marcia Whittaker walked directly across to Perry Mason, holding a manila envelope in her hand. When she got within two steps of the lawyer, she slid the manila envelope behind her back, and held it across the curve of her hips.

Mason said sharply, "Don't be like that!"

"I want to know," she said, "exactly what I'm going to get."

"A first-degree murder rap if you don't watch your step," he warned.

"You'll promise me that Alden Leeds will stand back of me, that . . ."

"I promise you nothing." Mason said. "I've gone too damn far already. Who do you think you are, to stand up there and ask me, will I do this and will I do that? You're standing on a red-hot spot." Mason pointed dramatically to the door. "Any minute the law may walk in through that door. If they find those papers on you, it means the gas chamber. And you want to know what I'm

70

going to do for you! For one thing, I'm going to take those papers off your hands. That's enough—too damn much."

She whipped the envelope from behind her back, and literally pushed it into his hands.

Without looking at it, Mason dropped it into his inside coat pocket. "I'm not your lawyer," he said. "I'm Alden Leeds' lawyer. To the extent that you play ball with him, I'll play ball with you. Try to slip anything over on him, and I'll give you the works. Do you understand?"

She nodded. There were tears in her eyes.

"Listen," Mason went on, "John Milicant was being shadowed. Private detectives kept a record of everyone who went to the sixth floor of that apartment. There's an elevator indicator over the elevator shaft. There are two other apartments on the sixth floor. At least one of them is vacant. Everyone who took the elevator up to the sixth floor was clocked in and clocked out."

"Who hired them?" she asked.

"I did," Mason said.

"Then can't you . . ."

"Not a chance in the world," Mason told her, "and I don't even dare to try. There were two men and two women on the job working in relays. You try to hush up anything like that, and you wind up in a lot hotter water than when you started."

"But what can I do?" she asked.

Mason said, "The apartment door was closed when you went in?"

"Yes, but I had a key to it."

"There's a spring lock on the door?"

"Yes."

Mason said, "Give me your key."

She crossed to the table where she had tossed her purse, opened it, took out a key and handed it to him. He dropped it in his pocket. "Forget that you ever had this," he told her. "Now, what did you do when you came out? Did you pull the door shut?"

"No. I left it part way open—just an inch or two."

71

"Why?"

"I was afraid that when the blow-off came, they might claim I'd been the last one in—and that I had a key. By leaving the door slightly ajar—someone else might come to see Louie, and push the door open, and find him, and be on a spot that would let me out."

Mason said, "You're a cold-blooded little devil, aren't you?"

"Christ, no!" she said. "I've always been too much the other way, but I've learned to think for myself in a jam. You would too, if you had them hand you the deals they've handed me."

Mason studied her with hard, watchful eyes. "You were wearing gloves?" he asked.

"Yes."

Mason nodded toward the telephone. "Call the police. Tell them you had a date with Louie Conway at his apartment, that he was to wait for you there, that you pounded and hammered on the door, and he didn't answer, that you know it isn't a stand-up because he was going to marry you, and you were going away together."

"If I just tell them that," she said, "they'll think I'm crazy."

Mason said, "That's what you want. Act crazy. Be hysterical over the telephone. Ask them to please send someone out to the apartment to make sure he's all right. Tell them you've been trying to sleep, and couldn't, that you knew he was afraid of something, that he'd been gambling, and he was afraid men were going to kidnap him. And don't, under any circumstances, mention the name of Milicant."

"But that won't do any good," she said.

"Don't you see?" Mason told her. "They'll make a record of that call and of your name and address. They'll hand you a line and tell you they'll have a radio car drop by for an inspection, that if you don't hear from them, it'll be all right."

"And they won't go?"

"Of course not. They can't go around hammering on the apartment doors of all the men in the city who have stood up trollops on dates. In the morning when the thing breaks, that call will get you as much in the clear as you can get. With that call, they'll never think of trying to check up on the airports."

Her tear-reddened eyes blinked as she digested the lawyer's advice.

"Then," Mason went on, "when the law does come, you'll have plenty of excuse for having had a sleepless night and putting on the weep act. Remember, you were to be married. The man's sister has been trying to break up the match."

"Should I bring her in?" she asked.

"Yes," Mason said. "All the way. Don't forget, Marcia, the records show you were in the apartment for *eleven minutes*.

"Get out of those clothes. Get into pajamas and litter this apartment with cigarette stubs. Have a drink of whiskey and leave the whiskey bottle and the glass out where the officers can find 'em. See that there are plenty of half-burnt cigarettes in the bedroom—not stubs, mind you, that would make you seem too calm. You want to register as having had one cigarette after another, with only a puff or two from each. Don't have any make-up on your face. Let your hair string down. Lie in bed long enough and turn around often enough to get the sheets all rumpled. Go into the kitchen, mix salt into a glassful of water. Sprinkle the salt water on the pillow so it'll be damp to the touch, but don't overdo it.

"Can you go through with it?"

"Yes," she said.

Mason took Della Street's arm.

Marcia Whittaker stood at the head of the stairs, sobbing silently as she waited for the front door to slam before switching out the light.

On the cold pavement in front of the house, with the first streaks of dawn showing in the east, Della Street turned anxious eyes to Perry Mason. "Chief," she asked, "aren't we doing a lot for Alden Leeds?"

Mason grinned down at her. "I'll say we are. Getting cold feet, Della?"

She snuggled her arm in his. "Be your age, you big oaf."

They drove a dozen blocks before Mason found an all-night

restaurant with a public telephone. He parked the car, went into the restaurant, and called Paul Drake's office. When he heard the detective's voice on the line, he said, "Okay, Paul. You can go home now," and hung up.

Chapter 8

Phyllis Leeds sat across from Mason in the big leather chair, her eyes darkened by apprehension and fear of what was to follow.

Mason said, "There's no way of breaking it gently, Miss Leeds, so brace yourself."

"About Uncle Alden?" she asked.

"Not directly," Mason said. "It's about John Milicant. He was found in his apartment about an hour ago by a maid. He'd been murdered."

"Murdered?"

Mason nodded. "A carving knife stuck in the back, a little above the left shoulder. The blade forward and downward."

"Good Heavens!" she exclaimed.

"Paul Drake had operatives on the job all last night," Mason went on. "We know everyone who entered the apartment house where Milicant had his apartment—everyone, that is, that went to the sixth floor. Among those persons was a Marcia Whittaker, whom John Milicant intended to marry, and a man who answers the description of your Uncle Alden."

"Uncle Alden!" she exclaimed. "That's impossible!"

Mason said, "So far we're working on incomplete data. I'm telling you what we have."

"But there's some mistake. It *couldn't* have been Uncle Alden."

"All right," Mason said, "we'll assume that it wasn't your Uncle Alden."

"The way you say it sounds as though you thought it *was* he."

Mason said quietly, "I think it was," and then went on, "The last person to enter that apartment was Marcia Whittaker. She *says* she found the apartment locked, that she

75

pounded on the door and got no answer. She waited around in the corridor for four or five minutes, calling John's name and tapping on the door. When he didn't answer, she finally left. She went back to her own flat, and, as I get the story, called police headquarters around five o'clock this morning, telling them she thought something was wrong and asking them to make an investigation. They made a very routine investigation. They keep the names of persons injured in automobile accidents and persons taken to the emergency hospitals. They checked through those lists and found no record of a Louie Conway—which was the name under which Marcia knew John Milicant. They naturally reached the conclusion that it was a stand-up and paid no further attention to it."

"Do you mean that John Milicant was Louie Conway . . . the one Uncle Alden made the check to? Did . . ."

As her voice trailed off into silence, Mason said, "Yes."

"I can't believe it. . . . Are you certain?"

"Marcia Whittaker says he was, and it looks like it. Have you heard anything from Ned Barkler?"

"No. He packed up and left, bag and baggage."

"He told me he was going," Mason said. "Tell me, do you know anything at all about a Bill Hogarty?"

She frowned. "Bill Hogarty," she repeated.

"Yes," Mason said, watching her closely.

"I've heard the name," she said, after a while. "I think I heard Ned Barkler and Uncle Alden talking about him once."

"Do you know what was said?"

"No. I remember now. They were talking in low tones when I came into the room. Barkler had his back turned to me. I heard him say, 'You got Hogarty's. . .' and then Uncle Alden frowned at him. He looked up and saw me, and quit talking."

"Do you know how long ago that was?"

"No, I don't. To tell you the truth, it didn't impress me much at the time. I thought . . ." She broke off and laughed nervously. "To tell you the truth, Mr. Mason, I thought I'd interrupted a smutty story. Have you told Emily? We must notify her."

Mason shook his head. "The police haven't been able to locate her."

"But where is she?" Phyllis Leeds asked.

"That," Mason said, "is what the police are interested in right now. She was at her brother's apartment about six o'clock last night."

"You mean the Conway apartment?"

"Yes."

"But I can't believe *she* knew that John was Conway."

"I don't think she knew it," Mason said, "—until yesterday afternoon. But when she found it out, she knew enough about Conway to know where to find him."

"How did she find out?"

"I told her."

"You did?"

"Yes."

"How did you know?"

"Putting two and two together," Mason said.

"Why didn't you tell me?"

"I didn't want to bother you with details or worry you. Look here, Miss Leeds. I have some information of the greatest value to your Uncle Alden. If he gets in touch with you, tell him that. Tell him to talk with me before he does a single thing or makes any statement to anyone. Do you understand?"

She nodded.

"All right," Mason said. "Go on home, sit tight, and don't worry. I'm not going to burden you with a lot of details. I'm doing everything I can do—but I'm working in the dark."

She rose obediently. "My head's spinning like a top," she said. "Why should Uncle Alden have given John Milicant twenty thousand dollars? Why should he have gone to see him? Why should . . ."

"Forget it," Mason interrupted. "Things will move fast from now on. Answers will be uncovered faster than you can think up questions. Go home, sit tight, and see that your Uncle Alden gets in touch with me. And if the police question you, make Ned Barkler's departure seem as casual as possible."

She walked slowly toward the door, then turned to flash him a quick smile. "With you on the job, I feel that I don't have to worry."

"That's the spirit," Mason told her. "I'll be on the job pretty much from now on."

Drake entered the office less than ten minutes after Phyllis Leeds had departed. "Perry," he asked suspiciously, "why did you want me to keep on the job last night and this morning and see if there were any unusual activities at Milicant's apartment?"

Mason met the detective's stare steadily. "Want me to tell you, Paul?" he asked.

"No," Drake said hastily. "Lord knows why I asked that question in the first place. It's just been sticking in my mind, that's all."

"Better get it out of your mind," Mason said. "What else do you know?"

"The police figure robbery was one of the motives for Milicant's murder. He always carried a wallet, and it was usually well filled. The wallet is gone. Someone certainly went through the apartment looking for something they may or may not have found. The place is a wreck."

"Anything else?" Mason asked. "How about time of death? Have they fixed that?"

"Tentatively at around ten-thirty, somewhere between ten and ten-forty-five."

Mason frowned. "Why the exactness?" he asked. "Good Lord, Paul, I could cite you cases by the dozen where the autopsy surgeons have missed the time of death by from twelve to twenty-four hours. Look at the New York case where the man killed the model."

"I know," Drake agreed, "but that's where they figure on body temperature, *rigor mortis*, and things like that. This case is different. There's no question on earth as to when he ate his dinner. Serle says they were discussing a business deal, and that he ordered up the dinner but can't remember what time it was. He thinks it was around eight-thirty, and that he didn't leave until around nine. But our men have clocked him in and clocked him out. What's more, the waiter over at the restaurant remembers the occasion perfectly. The dinner was delivered at eighten. It consisted of broiled lamb chops, green peas, and baked potato. Once the autopsy surgeon knows when a meal was eaten, if death occurs before the food has left the stomach, he can fix the time of death very accurately."

Mason hooked his thumbs through the armholes of his vest and started pacing the floor, his head thrust forward, eyes moodily contemplating the carpet. "That," he said, "dumps it right in Marcia Whittaker's lap."

Drake nodded.

"Or," Mason added, "on the shoulders of the old man."

Drake said, "By the way, Perry, there's no question about the identity of the old man. The police dug up a photograph of Leeds and showed it to my operatives. They identify it as being the photograph of the man who went up to that apartment."

Drake fed a couple of sticks of chewing gum into his mouth. The expression of his face remained calmly tranquil, but his jaw moved with nervous rapidity. After a moment, he said, "Milicant didn't have diabetes, did he, Perry?"

"Not that I know of. I may be able to find out. Why?"

"A peculiar condition of the right foot. Four of the toes had been amputated. The autopsy surgeon figures it was due to gangrene, but found no present indication of a diabetic condition."

Mason stared thoughtfully at Drake. "He walked with a slight limp," he said. "It never occurred to me to find out the reason."

Without changing the rhythm of his rapid gum-chewing, the detective nodded.

"You're making a search for Leeds?"

"Yes. We're checking on the airplanes—particularly those that went north."

Mason said, "I want to talk with Serle."

"Fat chance you'll stand," Drake said gloomily. "They've nailed him for conducting a lottery and selling lottery tickets. The police were looking for him at the very moment he was having dinner with Milicant."

"What was the idea of the conference with Milicant? Do you know, Paul?"

"Apparently in regard to raising bail. After he left Milicant's apartment, he told friends that he'd arranged to get cash bail and was going to surrender, that he could beat the rap hands down."

"Then what happened?" Mason asked, interested.

"He hung around a pool room for two or three hours, then put through a call to Conway."

"What time was that call?" Mason interrupted to ask.

"That's just it," Drake said. "We can't get the exact time. I've had men working on it, and so have the police."

"The police must be working fast," Mason said.

"You bet they're working fast," Drake agreed. "My man got a hot lead, and beat the police to it by only ten minutes."

"What did he find out, Paul?"

"Well, there are a couple of fellows who heard the conversation. One of them heard some of it, and another guy heard nearly all of it. Serle had told them he was supposed to call Conway around ten-thirty. He put through the call, and asked if everything was okay. Conway evidently told him it was. They talked for two or three minutes, and then Serle hung up. He played a game of pool for about ten minutes, then he called police headquarters, wanted to know what the hell they meant by raiding his joint, said his business was just as legal as any of the banknight schemes, and that he was going to prove it. He said he was coming up and surrender and make bail, and left right after that.

"Now, you can figure what that means. He had left Conway's apartment shortly after eight o'clock. Evidently Conway had agreed to raise bail for him. But the joker was that Conway didn't have the dough. He probably told Serle he knew where he could raise the money.

"You can see where it all ties in. Conway was blackmailing Alden Leeds. Leeds was to come up around ten o'clock—evidently with another twenty grand. With that money in his jeans, Conway was going to bail Serle out."

Mason, pacing the floor, said, "Paul, we've simply got to fix the time of that telephone call."

"I know it," Drake said. "If it was as late as ten-thirty, it will prove Milicant, or Conway, was alive after Leeds left."

Mason said, "Hell, Paul, it *must* have been either while Leeds was there, or right after he'd left. Conway must have told Serle that the dough was ready. Serle went down and gave himself up on the strength of it."

"Well," Drake said, "it's just one of those things. No one seems to have bothered about the exact time. Apparently, Serle doesn't have the time element fixed very clearly in his mind. He thought it was nearly nine o'clock before he left Conway's apartment. We know it was before eight-thirty. He was down at the pool room by nine o'clock. He said he was to call Conway around ten-thirty. The men who heard the telephone conversation think it was right around ten-thirty, but the point is, they aren't sure."

Mason said, "How about checking it the other way, Paul? The police records must show when Serle was booked."

"They do, but he gave himself up sometime before he was booked. Estimates vary from as little as five minutes to as much as twenty. He was booked at ten-fifty-five."

Mason said, "I've got to talk with Serle."

Drake said, "The cops hold all the trumps. Remember, they have a felony rap on Serle."

"What happened to his bail?" Mason asked.

"There wasn't any bail. It was fixed at five grand. Serle squawked his head off and tried to get it at a thousand, but they sat tight at five. By the time the argument was over, and Serle called for Conway to come down and put up the bail, it was around eleven-thirty. By that time, of course, there was no answer on the phone. Serle thought Conway had given him a double cross, and he was so damn mad he could hardly talk. He kept calling Conway's place until the cops threw him in the cooler. They won't let him out now until he's signed a written statement, and you can figure that statement ain't going to help *us* any."

Mason said, "Look here, Paul. Our only chance is to mix this thing all up, so the D.A. doesn't know just what to go after, and then grab the facts we want out of the scramble."

Drake nodded, but without enthusiasm. "It isn't going to be so easy, Perry," he said.

The telephone rang. Mason picked it up, said, "Hello," and Drake's secretary said, "Mr. Mason, would you mind passing the word on to Mr. Drake that operative number twelve telephoned in to report that Guy T. Serle is out walking the streets?"

"Thanks," Mason said, "I will. Was there anything else?"

"No, just that," she said.

Mason hung up the telephone, and said, "Serle's out.—That was your office on the line."

"Where did the report originate?" Drake asked.

"Your operative twelve."

Drake said, "Well, there you are, Perry. They could have thrown the book at him a dozen different ways. He's out walking the streets. That means he did just what the D.A. wanted him to."

Mason said, "I want to get in touch with this bird. How can we fix it up so it seems casual?"

"We can't," Drake said.

"Sure we can," Mason insisted. "What are his personal habits? How well do you know them?"

"We've covered him up one side and down the other," Drake said.

Mason looked at his watch, drummed with his fingers, and abruptly inquired, "Does he eat lunch, Paul?"

"I'll say he does. He's a great eater, likes his food, and eats plenty of it."

"Where do you suppose he'll eat lunch today?"

Drake took a notebook from his pocket, opened it, and thumbed through the pages. "Here we are," he said. "Complete data on the guy. . . . H'mmmmm. . . . Let me see where he eats. . . . Here it is. Most of the time at the Home Kitchen Cafe down on East Ranchester. It's only a couple of blocks from where he was running the business."

"What does he look like?"

Drake read a description from the book. "Around forty, an even six feet, hundred and sixty pounds, gray eyes, long, straight nose, thin features, red hair, thin lips, always wears double-breasted suits."

"Why should a bird who likes his grub eat at a dump on East Ranchester?" Mason asked.

"Because it's a swell place to eat, Perry. My operatives looked it up. It's run by a French couple. Serle kids one of the waitresses quite a bit, and she seems to like him."

"Got her name?" Mason asked.

Drake turned over the page, ran his forefinger down the notes, and said, "Sure. . . . Here it is. . . . Hazel Stickland."

"Does she figure in it?" Mason asked.

"I don't think so. I told my men to collect everything they could on the bird, and they went to town."

Mason said, "Think I'll drop in there for lunch."

"You *might* land him that way," Drake said, "but it wouldn't fool him any."

"I'm not so certain I care about fooling him, Paul. He . . ."

The door from the outer office opened, and Della Street came breezing in. "Hi, Paul," she said, by way of greeting. "How's the sleep?"

Drake groaned. "Not worth mentioning, and I'm headed back to put my nose to the grindstone. . . . So long."

When he had gone, Mason said to Della Street, "What did the handwriting expert say?"

"He'll try and get us a preliminary report just as soon as possible. It's not a report that he'd swear to, but it'll be something you can bank on just the same. What was in the envelope, Chief, and why did you rush it over to the expert?"

Mason said, "An omelet that I can't unscramble. Photostatic copies of hotel registers back in October of 1907, the Regina Hotel at Dawson, the Golden North Hotel at Skagway, a hotel at White Horse, and one in Seattle."

"What do they show?"

"The signatures of Bill Hogarty."

"What else?" she asked.

"There was a letter written by Leeds to John Milicant, dated thirty days ago, stating that he had never heard of Mr. B. C. Hogar, and that if Mr. Hogar presumed to give him a reference, it was an indication that Hogar would stand investigation. There was an old yellowed newspaper clipping from a Dawson paper telling about the finding of a body in the Tanana district. The body showed evidence of violence. The clipping doesn't state specifically what was found. It goes on to say that the body had been tentatively identified as that of an Alden Leeds who had been in partnership with a Bill Hogarty and was reputed to have struck it rich, that Hogarty had left the Klondike district in the fall of 1907 after coming upstream from the Tanana district. He had been traced as far as Seattle where he had married a girl who had been employed in the *'M and N Dance Hall'* at Dawson. At this late date—the article was dated 1912—the police had been unable to find any further trace of either party."

Della Street frowned. "What does that add up to, Chief?"

"I don't know," Mason said. "There were a lot of other things, photographs, location notices, things which had evidently been collected with the greatest care."

"And who's B. C. Hogar?" she asked.

Mason smiled and said, "He might be Bill Hogarty under another name."

"Then the first initial would be 'W,' " she said. "Bill is a nickname for William."

Mason nodded. "And, on the other hand," he went on, "it might be that someone who suspected rather strongly that Alden Leeds was in reality Bill Hogarty, wanted him to sign the name, 'Bill Hogarty,' for the purpose of checking handwriting, but naturally he was afraid to let the cat out of the bag, so he wrote a letter asking information about a B. C. Hogar, and Leeds, without suspecting what was in the wind, answered the letter in such a way that he wrote the name not only once but twice."

The telephone rang. Mason looked at his wrist watch and

said, "I'll bet Stive has a golf engagement this afternoon and broke his neck to get an opinion in just before twelve."

He lifted the receiver, said, "Hello," and Gertrude Lade, at the switchboard, asked, "Do you want to talk with Mr. Stive, the handwriting expert?"

"Put him on," Mason said.

A moment later, Milton Stive said, "Hello, Mason. I can't give you a lot of reasons backing up my conclusion as yet, but the letter dated last month was written by the same person who signed the hotel registers 'Bill Hogarty.' "

"You're certain?" Mason asked.

"A good handwriting expert offers only his opinion," Stive said, "but in this instance it's virtually a mathematical certainty. There are, of course, certain allowances to be made for the lapse of time. There has evidently been an interval of thirty-two years in the signatures. A man's handwriting naturally changes, particularly when the thirty-two years' lapse carries over the period of greatest physical efficiency. We naturally would expect to find the curves more angular, the style a little more cramped, but, making proper allowances for that, the similarity between the capital 'B' in the 'Bill' and a comparison of the word 'Hogar' and 'Hogarty' remove any possible doubt. I have photographed one of the Hogarty signatures, and have photographed the name 'Hogar,' on an exactly identical scale. I have then superimposed the two photographs, and there is more than a similarity. There is a virtual identity."

Mason shot Della Street a swift wink. "When can you give me a complete written opinion, Stive?" he asked.

Stive cleared his throat. "Well," he said, "not before Monday evening at the earliest. It would require a great deal of work. In addition to that, it would be necessary to make certain photographs and . . ."

Mason interrupted with a laugh. "Oh, go ahead and shoot your golf, you big bluff, and don't breathe a word of this to anyone."

Mason hung up the receiver, said to Della Street, "I'm going out and try to locate Serle, Della. I think he'll eat at the Home

Kitchen Cafe. Stick around the office, keep in touch with developments, and eat after I get back."

"Okay, Chief. How about the outer office?"

"Close it up," Mason said. "Give Phyllis Leeds a ring after a while just to let her know we're on the job. Don't tell her anything that she couldn't read in the newspapers. Ask her if she knew John Milicant had a crippled foot, and see if she knows how it happened."

Chapter 9

Perry Mason, sitting at the corner table in the Home Kitchen Cafe, surveyed the restaurant in shrewd appraisal.

A sign announced that the restaurant opened at seven o'clock A.M. and closed at seven-thirty P.M. Placards, placed on the wall, listed a series of tempting breakfast combinations. Particular inducements were made to secure regular patronage.

There was a lunch counter running half the length of the restaurant on one side. At the front end of this was a well-stocked cigar counter and a large cash register presided over by a genial, fat man whose lips were held in a good-natured grin of easy affability. His bald head shone like a freshly peeled onion in the light reflected from the plate-glass window at the front of the restaurant. His eyes were quick, and keen as those of a hawk.

Opposite the lunch counter were tables capable of seating four, and along the wall were a number of booths. Fast-moving, capable waitresses in clean, starched dresses darted swiftly about. Everywhere was an atmosphere of well-oiled, clock-like efficiency.

A waitress approached Mason to take his order. The lawyer smiled, handed her two one-dollar bills, and said, "I'm giving you the tip before I eat. I'm waiting for a party. Do you happen to know a man named Serle?"

She hesitated over taking the tip.

"A tall, thin chap around forty," Mason said.

Again she shook her head.

"He's friendly with a waitress named Hazel."

"Oh, I know the man you mean."

"If he comes in for lunch," Mason said, "tell him that Perry Mason, the lawyer, wants to see him and point me out to him."

"Is that all?" she asked.

Mason said, "That's all."

She took the two dollars, and said, somewhat dubiously, "Suppose he doesn't want to see you?"

"Then," Mason said with a grin, "I'll see him."

She smiled and left him.

Not more than ten minutes later, Mason saw a man who answered Serle's description enter the restaurant, nod to the proprietor, and start for a table. The waitress whom Mason had tipped glided swiftly toward him. Mason, turning his profile, devoted himself to a cigarette. A few seconds later, he turned around—casually.

Guy T. Serle was approaching his table.

Mason nodded without eagerness and indicated a chair with a wave of his hand.

"So you're Mason," Serle said, his eyes showing quick interest. "I've heard about you. . . . I don't need a mouthpiece."

"I don't solicit business," Mason told him.

Quick comprehension showed in Serle's eyes. "And *I'm* not talking about that other matter," he said.

"Why not?" Mason asked.

"I'm a witness for the prosecution."

"That doesn't keep one from telling the facts."

"It does me."

"Been ordered not to talk?" Mason asked.

Serle shrugged his shoulders, caught the eye of a waitress, and beckoned to her. As she crossed over to the table, Serle asked, "Where's Hazel?"

She said, "Hazel's not here today."

Serle frowned. "Her day off?" he asked.

The waitress shook her head.

"Well, where is she?" Serle demanded.

"I don't know. I guess she's gone. It was her morning to open up. She didn't show, and the boss got sore. I wasn't supposed to come on until eleven, and he got me up out of my beauty sleep.

88

He telephoned Hazel's rooming house, and they said she'd left before midnight last night, took a suitcase with her, and beat it."

"Beat it?" Serle echoed.

"Uh huh—and her room rent's paid up until the first, and today's payday. She has a week's wages coming—fat chance she stands of getting them now. What's your order?"

"Lunch," Serle said shortly.

Placing silverware, a butter dish, and a glass of water before Serle, she glanced at the place which had been set in front of Mason at the table, and asked, "How about you? Ready to give your order now?"

Mason nodded. She handed him a menu, and Serle said, "If you want some good eats, just order lunch."

Mason smiled. "Just bring me the lunch."

When the waitress had left, Mason said, conversationally, "What were you and Milicant talking about?"

"Milicant?" Serle repeated questioningly. "Oh, yes, I keep forgetting his name was Milicant. I knew him as Louie Conway."

"What were you talking about?" Mason asked.

Serle said, "Listen, Mason, I'm not foolish enough to talk my way into the cooler."

Mason said, "The D.A. can't square your rap."

"I'll take a chance," Serle said. "Anyway, they have nothing on me. I have a legitimate business. I don't know whether the people who buy stuff I sell are stage magicians or whether they intend to start gambling. I always warn them it's a crime to introduce fraud into a gambling game. That lets me out. I've done my duty."

"How about the lottery?" Mason asked.

"There wasn't any lottery. I don't know where you heard that."

"The D.A. can't square a federal rap."

"What are you leading up to?"

"Where a man writes a letter and says, 'I can't deliver you the stuff you ordered by mail, but you'll get it by special messenger,' it's the same as using the mails in the business."

The waitress appeared with two bowls of pearl barley soup.

"What did you mean by that last crack?" Serle asked.

"Nothing," Mason said, munching a cracker.

"Listen, Mason," Serle said. "Get me straight on this. That lottery business is the bunk. I was closed up on a tip-off. It was a grudge tip-off. The D.A. doesn't go for that stuff. He doesn't use his office to settle private grudges. What's more, you can't convict a man on a tip-off. You've got to have evidence."

"That's right," Mason agreed.

There was another long silence while Mason finished his soup. Serle watched him uneasily. Mason pushed the plate away and said, "Nice soup."

Serle said, "Understand this, Mason, I don't think Leeds killed him, but the D.A. thinks so, and the D.A. has a case so airtight you couldn't punch a hole in it with a drill."

"What makes it airtight?" Mason asked.

Serle said, "I'm not talking."

"Is that the price you had to pay for squaring the rap with the D.A.?" Mason asked.

Serle said, "There isn't any rap."

The waitress brought a fruit salad, a plate of delicious meat pie made with tender squares of meat, rich, yellow carrots, new potatoes, walnut-sized onions, and steaming gravy.

"Certainly is fine grub," Mason said, appreciatively inhaling the aroma of the food.

"Look here," Serle said, "I'm not supposed to do any talking to anyone, newspapermen or anyone."

"In return for having that lottery business squared?" Mason asked.

"Quit harping about that," Serle said irritably. "There isn't any evidence on the sale of any lottery tickets."

Mason said, "If you don't mind, Serle, I'm going to sop this bread in the gravy. Certainly has a wonderful flavor. Are all their dishes this good?"

"They specialize in home cooking. Look here, Mason, you can't pull this stuff with me."

"What stuff?" Mason asked.

"Trying to shake me down. Hell, don't think I was born yesterday. All I've got to do is to step over to that phone, ring the district attorney, and tell him the defense lawyer is trying to tamper with one of his witnesses, and they'll have you on the spot so fast you won't have a chance to finish your dinner."

Mason gravely handed him a dime. "There's the phone," he said. "Hop to it."

"I'm not that kind," Serle said. "I don't squeal."

Mason said, "Of course, if the district attorney wanted actual proof, I could see that he had the lottery ticket and the crooked crap dice which you delivered for twenty-five bucks to Paul Drake."

Serle, who had been about to attack his meat pie, paused with the fork poised over the plate. "What the hell are you trying to pull?" he asked.

Mason speared a carrot, cut a corner from the rich crust of the pie, and conveyed it to his mouth. After watching Serle, Mason said, "Drake's the head of the Drake Detective Agency. He was working for me."

Serle said, "Oh," tonelessly.

"We were trying to locate Conway," Mason said. "We found out about the Conway Appliance Company, but it had moved. We couldn't get the post office to kick loose with a forwarding address so we sent twenty-five bucks on a chance. The chance paid off."

He returned to his meat pie.

"Look here," Serle said abruptly, "what do you want?"

"The low-down," Mason said.

Serle pushed back his plate. "I'll have to call a party," he said.

"Someone at the D.A.'s office?" Mason asked.

"No."

"Who?"

"Just a party."

"Go ahead and call," Mason said.

Serle was closeted in the telephone booth for nearly ten minutes. "All right, Mason," he said, returning to the table, "I have a free hand."

Mason smiled. "So have I."

Serle sat down. "Look here, Mason. Suppose I give you a break in this thing. What's in it for me?"

Mason said, "I'll let you pay my luncheon check."

Serle frowned, and said, "I'm not kidding."

"Neither am I."

"All right then, you had your chance and you've lost it."

Serle attacked his half-cold meat pie with savage haste.

Mason finished his salad, cleaned up his plate, lit a cigarette, and sipped coffee.

"Dessert?" the waitress asked.

"Bring me ice cream," Mason said, "and the check to him," indicating Serle.

Serle scraped his plate and pushed it back with a gesture of irritation.

"Your food won't agree with you eating hastily that way," Mason cautioned.

Serle said, "This is a hell of a way to act. I had to talk my head off in order to get a free hand, and now *you* start getting hard."

Mason said, "I'm always hard," and moved back to let the waitress scrape crumbs from the tablecloth.

Serle said, in a surly voice, "Bring me apple pie à la mode, and lots of coffee."

"Yes, sir," the waitress said and moved away.

Mason hitched his chair around so he was sitting sideways to the table, crossed his long legs, and smoked with every evidence of enjoyment.

"You couldn't drag that in on cross-examination anyway," Serle said.

"Oh, you'd be surprised at what a good lawyer can do on cross-examination," Mason observed affably. "You can ask a man a lot of embarrassing questions. You can impeach his veracity. You can show that he's been convicted of a felony and . . ."

"Well, I haven't been convicted of any felony," Serle snapped.

"No," Mason told him with a smile, "but you could be before the case came to trial. The federal men work fast, and murder cases usually drag along . . . particularly when a lawyer has some reason for dragging 'em along."

Serle said, with a burst of temper, "I smelled a rat on the Drake remittance right after we'd made delivery. I'd just taken over the business. I didn't know all of the customers. He wrote a letter which led me to believe . . ." His voice trailed away into sulky silence.

"I know," Mason said. "Tough, isn't it? A man always hates to go to jail thinking he's been a sucker."

Serle said, "I'm not a sucker."

"You're being one right now," Mason said.

The waitress brought their dessert. Mason started eating his ice cream. Serle pushed his pie to one side, and said, "Oh, all right! Have it your own way. I'd known Louie off and on for several years. He picked up the agency for this loaded dice business. I'd worked out a sweepstakes proposition. I figured I could combine 'em. Louie wouldn't sell me an interest.

"Then Louie wanted to get out. He told me he'd made a killing, had picked up twenty grand on the first installment, and said he was going to get a hundred before he quit."

"Blackmail?" Mason asked.

"What do *you* think?"

"I'm not thinking," Mason said, finishing his ice cream. "I'm listening."

"Of course, it was blackmail! It was a sweet hookup."

"Know what he had on Leeds?" Mason asked.

"Of course not. You don't think Louie was *that* simple, do you? When a man has a gold mine, he doesn't give his friends a chance to jump the claim.

"Well, I bought the business. I thought it would be a good thing to move it, but I kept the name because it was a mail-order business."

"Go ahead," Mason told him.

"The law raided my dump. I was out. They picked up a lot of incriminating stuff, but couldn't prove any deliveries. My assistant was smart enough to dump the tickets where they'd be absolutely safe."

"The officers will pick up your mail as it comes in," Mason said.

Serle laughed. "That's what *you* think. As soon as I heard about it, I beat it to the post office the very first thing and left a change of address. There won't be a single letter come into the dump."

"Nice going," Mason observed.

Serle looked pleased with himself.

"Then what?" Mason asked.

"Then, of course, I went to Conway. I was sore. I thought he'd sold me something hot."

"What did Conway say?" Mason asked.

"Conway was worried. He said he'd bail me out, that the thing had been clean as a hound's tooth when he sold it to me. Naturally, I told him it was Leeds that was responsible for the police tip-off. He said it couldn't be. I told him it was, and that it was up to him to square the rap."

"Just what did Conway say?" Mason asked.

"He said, 'Tell you what you do, Guy. Hide out until I have a chance to get things fixed up the way I want 'em. It'll probably take me a couple of hours, but it may be a little sooner. Give me a ring, and I'll let you know when to come up. Then you come up to my apartment, and we'll talk things over.' I told him I didn't want to talk things over, I wanted action. He told me to come up, and I'd get action."

"So you went up?" Mason asked.

"Yes, I went up. I was pretty nervous. Louie was busy as a one-armed paper hanger, answering the telephone, and scribbling a bunch of figures. Neither of us had eaten, and Louie gave me the number of a restaurant and told me to have some grub sent up. He said he could only give me a few minutes while we were eating. He said he was putting over a couple of big deals.

"While we were guzzling grub, Louie said to me, 'Now listen, Guy. I dropped most of that twenty grand I made in the touch from Leeds, but I'm resourceful and I stick by my friends. Now I don't want you to know anything about this—it wouldn't be good for you—but a party's going to be in here a little before ten with some dough—lots of it. Now, suppose you call me up and get an okay to be sure there's no hitch. Then go down to jail, be booked, put up a cash bond, and walk right out.' "

Mason stared at the tip of his cigarette. "You say Louie had a lot of other things he was doing?" he asked.

"Yes. The phone rang two or three times, and he put in a couple of calls."

"What were they?" Mason asked.

Serle said, "I can't help you much there. I had my own problems to worry about. Some of it was dope on the horses. Some of it wasn't. I remember he told somebody that things had been all settled up, and there wasn't going to be any trouble. He said, 'Why don't you come on down, and let me talk it over with you?' And then he said, 'Well, I could run up for just a minute. I don't want to be away more than a minute or two, but I can run up if you want.' And then he said, 'Well, that's all right then. You come down, but don't do it before ten o'clock. I'm going to be busy until after ten o'clock.' "

"Anything else?" Mason asked.

"There were lots of calls. I can't remember all of them. One of them was from his girl. She seemed to be all steamed up about something, and he was trying to smooth her over with a lot of yes-yes stuff. Hell, Mason, I can't remember all that junk. If I'd known he was going to get bumped off, I'd have listened, but all I wanted was to find out where *I* stood."

"Go on from there," Mason said.

"That's about all there is to it," Serle told him. "I left there right after we'd eaten, went down to a poolroom I knew, and hung around there until ten o'clock, then I called Louie, and he said everything was okay, that he'd stick around and wait for me to call from the station, jump in a cab, come down and put up the bail, and that would be all there was to it."

"Did you call the police immediately after that?" Mason asked.

"No, I didn't. I wanted a little time to go over what I was

going to tell the law. I played a game of pool and figured things out. I can think better while I'm knocking the ball around."

"What time did you call Louie?" Mason asked.

"Right around ten o'clock."

"As late as ten-thirty?" Mason asked, casually.

"Hell, no, it was ten o'clock. Christ, he told me to call at ten, and I called at ten. When a guy's going to put up the cash to spring you on a felony rap, you don't let half an hour slip through your fingers."

Mason said coldly, "Serle, you're lying. You called him around ten-thirty. You didn't remember the exact time. The first time you told your story, you admitted it. But after you'd talked with Homicide and seen they wanted to fix the call *before* Leeds had left, you decided to oblige them. You figured you could square your rap if you were obliging."

Serle said doggedly, "It was ten o'clock when I called. . . . They say Leeds is a multimillionaire."

"So I hear," Mason said.

"Maybe this is going to be kind of important to him," Serle suggested. "He might want to do something for me."

Mason met his eyes in cold, steady appraisal.

The waitress approached, said hurriedly to Mason, "You're Perry Mason?"

He nodded.

"There's a call for you from your office. They said it's *very* important, to get you at once."

Mason gestured toward Serle with a sweep of his hand. "Give him the check," he said, "with my compliments."

He strode to the telephone booth. Della Street was on the line. "Listen, Chief," she said, breathlessly. "Drake's located Alden Leeds."

"Where?"

"Seattle. Emily Milicant's with him. Drake's Seattle correspondent is keeping him under surveillance. Your plane leaves in thirty minutes. Think you can make it? I've got your reservation. I'll wire you all the details care of the Portland airport."

Mason said, "I'll make it. Take this in shorthand."

"Okay. Shoot."

"Milicant's apartment was on the sixth floor. Check everyone who had apartments above him. Serle let something slip about a conversation Milicant had over the phone. It may have been with someone above him in the same apartment house. Tell Drake a waitress named Hazel Stickland of the Home Kitchen Cafe took a runout powder. Have him check on that waiter who took the food up to Milicant's apartment. We're taking this waiter's story too much for granted. Find out if he knows this waitress. Have Drake try to find Hazel. Serle's sold us out to the D.A., lock, stock, and barrel. He fixes that conversation at ten o'clock. He knows he's lying, but he figures he can square his own pinch that way. Alden Leeds probably telephoned police the tip-off that got Serle's place raided. Milicant knew that when Leeds called, Leeds probably left another twenty grand with Milicant when he paid that last visit. Milicant must have been killed almost immediately after that. . . . Give all that dope to Paul Drake. Got it?"

"Got it," she said. "Happy landings, Chief."

Mason hung up and sprinted out of the restaurant.

Chapter 10

It was drizzling when Mason entered the Seattle Hotel. "You have a J. E. Smith here?" he asked.

The clerk verified the registration, and said, "Yes. Three-nineteen. Shall I give him a ring?"

Mason said slowly, "No, I'll call him after I've freshened up a bit. I had to leave in a hurry. Any place around here where I can get some clean clothes?"

"The middle of the next block," the clerk said. "They'll be open for an hour yet. Tomorrow's Sunday. Everything will be closed."

Mason nodded. "I want two rooms," he said, "one for myself, one for Mrs. George L. Manchester of New York. I'll pay for both rooms in advance. Give me the key to the room you select for Mrs. Manchester. I'll look it over, see if it's okay, and leave the key at the desk when I come down."

Mason took a billfold from his pocket and slid a twenty-dollar bill across the desk to the clerk, then signed his name and that of Mrs. George Manchester on the registration card the clerk handed him.

The bellboy took Mason to his room. The Manchester room was three doors away and on the other side of the corridor. When the bellboy had left, Mason took the stairs to the third floor and knocked on the door of 319.

Emily Milicant's voice asked sharply, "Who is it?"

"Express package," Mason said gruffly.

There was a moment of silence, then the rustle of motion, and the door opened a cautious inch.

Mason pushed it open. Emily Milicant fell back in dismay. A white-haired, thin man with cold, gimlet eyes, seated in an

98

overstuffed chair by the radiator, frowned at Mason. "Who the hell are you?" he asked.

Emily Milicant answered the question. "Perry Mason, the lawyer."

The man in the chair said, "Lock the door."

As Emily Milicant locked the door, Leeds asked, "How'd you find us?"

"Easy," Mason said. "Too easy. If I found you, the police can find you."

Emily Milicant, speaking rapidly, said, "Alden was simply terrified by that sanitarium. He was afraid he was going to be railroaded into an insane asylum. So he decided to run away."

Mason, seating himself on the bed, calmly appropriated pillows with which to bolster his back. He lit a cigarette, and said conversationally to Alden Leeds, "When did you last see John Milicant?"

Leeds said, "It's been about a week, I guess."

"Try again," Mason said.

Leeds stared at Mason, his cold, gray eyes, under frosty eyebrows, boring steadily into the lawyer's. "I don't understand," he said.

Mason said, "You called on John Milicant at ten-five last night."

"I don't know what you're talking about."

"You called on him where he'd had an apartment under the name of L. C. Conway," Mason said.

Emily Milicant started to say something, then stopped suddenly.

Mason went on casually, "Don't tell me that you don't know John Milicant was murdered last night sometime between ten and ten-forty-five."

Emily Milicant came to her feet, her eyes staring. "John!" she cried, and then, after a moment, "Murdered!"

Alden Leeds started to get to his feet, dropped back in the chair, and said sharply, "He's lying, Emily, trying to get something out of you. Don't fall for it."

Mason fished in his inside pocket, took out a clipping, hastily

99

torn from an early edition of the afternoon paper. He passed it across to Emily Milicant who read a few lines and crossed over to kneel beside Alden Leeds' chair. Together they read the newspaper account.

Mason said to Leeds, "You may or may not know that I've been employed to represent you by Phyllis."

"He knows," Emily Milicant said quickly. "Oh, Mr. Mason, this is awful . . . not that I didn't expect it would happen some day. I've told him time and time again that he must quit associating with . . ."

"Forget all that stuff," Mason interrupted roughly. "I don't know how much time we have. Not much, I'm afraid. Milicant was your brother. Under the name of Conway, he'd been blackmailing Alden Leeds. You, Leeds, went up to John Milicant's apartment last night. You were there at just about the time the murder must have been committed. The apartment was searched. It looks as though you're the one who did the searching. Now, never mind lies, tears, or sentiment. Shoot fast and shoot clean."

Leeds said, "I left there at nine-forty-five."

"Guess again," Mason said. "Private detectives were keeping the place under surveillance. You were clocked in at five minutes past ten and out at ten-sixteen."

Emily Milicant, wiping tears from her eyes, said, quietly, "That's right, Alden, it was ten-twenty-five when he called me and told me that you'd just left."

Mason's eyes bored steadily into hers. "He called you?" he asked.

"Yes."

"On the telephone?"

"Yes, of course."

"Where?"

"At my . . . at a number I'd given him where he could call me."

"Not at your apartment?" Mason asked.

"No."

Alden Leeds said slowly, "Until yesterday afternoon, I had no idea L. C. Conway and John Milicant were one and the same. I thought John Milicant was acting as my friend. He told me that he knew Conway, that Conway was a crook, but that he could handle him.

"I gave John Milicant a check for twenty thousand. The check was payable to Conway, and endorsed so Conway would accept it. John said Conway wouldn't go to the bank himself."

Emily Milicant said confidently, "And then last night, John gave you back the money, didn't he, Alden?"

"Gave me back the money!" Leeds said in surprise. "I should say not. Last night, he wanted *more* money."

"Wanted more money!" Emily exclaimed. "Why, he promised me that he was going to return the money to you."

Alden Leeds said dryly, "He gave me an ultimatum last night, told me I had to have another twenty thousand within twenty-four hours. I gave him fifteen more in cash."

Emily Milicant sat staring at him with wide, surprised eyes. "Why, he called me last night, just after you'd left, and told me everything had been fixed up, and that he'd returned all but two thousand dollars to you."

Leeds said nothing.

"Look here," Mason interrupted, "if you're absolutely certain your brother telephoned you at ten-twenty-five, it puts Alden Leeds in the clear."

"Of course, he did."

"You're certain it was your brother?"

"Of course. I guess I know my own brother's voice."

Mason said thoughtfully, "And how about your watch? Was it right?"

"It was right to the second," she said. "Alden and I were taking the midnight plane."

Mason said, "If that's the truth, Alden Leeds is in the clear."

"Of course, it's the truth. Why should I lie?"

"To help Alden Leeds, of course," Mason said. "Surely you don't expect the district attorney's going to quit cold simply on your say-so."

"Look here, Mr. Mason, I think Marcia was going to see

John. I think she was . . . was planning on spending the night with him."

"Who's Marcia?" Alden Leeds asked.

"A girl John was going to marry," Emily Milicant said. "I opposed the match, not because I thought she wasn't good enough for John, but because I *knew* John wasn't good enough for her. I knew it was a passing infatuation with John, and that he'd break her heart. I couldn't tell Marcia all I knew about John, so I had to pretend that I was opposing the match because I was prejudiced against *her*. Why, John would have broken her heart inside two months. He'd have dragged her down and down and down. That's what he's done to all of his women."

"He's dead," Mason pointed out.

"I don't care whether he's dead or not, " she blazed indignantly. "John Milicant was a mental defective. He couldn't differentiate between right and wrong, and he didn't even try."

"Ever been in prison?" Mason asked.

"Of course, he's been in prison. He served five years in the penitentiary at Waupun, Wisconsin. That was years ago."

"Then they'll have his fingerprint record," Mason said.

She shook her head. "He became a trusty in the prison office and was shrewd enough to get hold of his own fingerprints and substitute them," she said. "He got ten convicts to each donate a fingerprint. That confused his record so nothing could be done about it. It was before the days of a central fingerprint filing system. . . ."

Mason frowned thoughtfully. "Before he'd lost his toes?" he asked.

"He lost his toes at Waupun," she said. "Blood poisoning set in from an infected blister. They had to amputate four toes on his right foot."

Mason, studying her thoughtfully, said, "He was really your brother?"

"Of course, he was my brother."

"You're certain you hadn't assumed the relationship for the purpose of—traveling together?"

She flushed. "Certainly not," she snapped.

102

Mason turned to Alden Leeds. "Okay," he said, "Conway and John Milicant were one and the same. He was blackmailing you. What was the hold he had on you?"

"We won't go into that," Leeds said.

"I think we will, " Mason told him. "What's going to happen when the police find those papers in Conway's apartment?"

"What papers?"

Mason said, "I'm not going to show my hand until you've shown yours. I have enough to know whether you're telling me the truth. Suppose you start."

Leeds said, "I have no further statement to make."

Mason said, "Suppose I make one then. You're not Alden Leeds. You're really Bill Hogarty, who assumed Leeds' identity back in 1907."

Emily Milicant said, "Go ahead and tell him, Alden. Can't you see? Its the *only* way."

"We haven't got all night, you know," Mason prodded.

Leeds tamped tobacco down in his pipe. "I'll tell him about me, and leave you out of it, Emily," he said.

"Don't be silly," Emily Milicant retorted. "Tell him the whole thing."

He shook his head.

"All right. *I'll* tell him about *me*," she said. She turned to Perry Mason. "I was a dance hall girl," she went on. "I went up into the Klondike as a dancer for the *'M and N.'* That was before the days of taxi dancers as we know them nowadays. Dance hall girls were all kinds, straight and crooked. I was filled with the spirit of adventure, and wanted to go places and do things. Well, I went places, and I did things, and I'm not ashamed of anything I ever did.

"They told me when I left Seattle, I could work in the dance hall and be straight. I could, but I couldn't make any money at it. I'm no angel, but I never in my life gave myself to a man just for money. I was nineteen when I went up to the Klondike in 1906. That makes me fifty-two years old now. Now then, Alden, you go on from there."

Alden Leeds said, "I went into the Yukon in 1906. I picked

103

up a partner by the name of Hogarty. We went up in the Tanana district, and made a pretty good strike. Hogarty had got acquainted with Emily coming in on the boat. He fell for her hard, and kept writing to her.

"Emily went into the dance hall, and didn't like it. She decided to quit and buy an interest in a claim. Bill wrote her to come on up, and he thought he could get my consent to selling her a third interest in our claim.

"She came up. I'll never forget how Emily looked when I first saw her in our cabin. I looked at her, and fell head over heels in love with her.

"We'd been working hard. Our nerves were raw. I cussed Bill for bringing a good girl into the rough mining country. Bill told me to mind my own business. One word led to another, and, after two days, we weren't speaking. Emily tried to patch things up. The more she tried, the worse things got.

"It wasn't real cold yet, although there was frost in the air, and it was commencing to get dark. You know, it's light all night up there during the summer. Bill and I had moved out, and let Emily have the cabin. We slept out back, on balsam boughs—sleeping together for warmth, and neither one of us speaking. We woke up one morning, and found Emily gone. She'd left a note, saying that she saw it wouldn't work out, and she was on her way, that we weren't to try to follow.

"That didn't keep us from trying to follow. It didn't do us any good. We couldn't locate her. We came back to the claim, and went back to mining. Bill wanted to tear my throat out, and I wanted to tear his out. Then, one day we struck it rich. We stood and stared at each other over the big pile of gold, and Bill said, 'If it hadn't been for you, Emily would have had a share in this.' I called him a fighting name, and we mixed all over the place. Neither of us won. I was older and more solid. He was younger and faster. When we couldn't fight any more, we went into the cabin and put cold water on our faces. Then we went out and grubbed out more gold. We had an awful pile of it.

"That night Bill decide to kill me. I read it in his eyes. He figured that with me dead, he could take all of the gold and go get

104

Emily. He'd sensed by that time that she cared more for me than she did for him.

"We had a revolver and a rifle. I stuck the rifle down my pants leg and smuggled it out of the cabin when I went out to get wood. I left it where it would be handy. I was watching Bill like a hawk.

"About eight o'clock that night, it happened. He'd been drinking pretty heavy, and, all of a sudden, he straightened up and threw the whiskey bottle to one side. I read murder in his eyes. I think he wanted to say something, but he couldn't talk. He twisted his lips, and that was all. I was headed for the door by the time he'd raised the gun. Remember, I'd been waiting for just that play.

"Bill was fast. He shot twice, and missed both times. I ran around the cabin, and he after me. I had enough of a head start to keep the cabin between me and him. I grabbed the rifle, and shot.

"There I was, with a dead partner, out in the middle of the north country, a claim that was lousy with gold, and winter coming on. I knew it was a pocket. I knew it might play out to-morrow or next day or the next week, or, maybe, next season. But it was a pocket. If I left the claim to go and report to the authorities, and some prospector came along, he'd clean out the gold.

"I did the only thing that seemed logical at the time. I dragged Bill out a ways from the cabin, dug a hole, and buried him. It was exactly what he'd have done with me. I went back and stayed with that pocket. It petered out in about ten days. I had a fortune in gold. It took me five trips, lugging all I could carry, to get it down to the boat.

"Well, there I was. The river was due to start freezing almost any time. I had a big load of gold, and quite a few people knew my partner was Bill Hogarty. I couldn't explain Bill's absence without getting into a lot of trouble. I didn't dare to lie about it, and I didn't dare to tell the truth.

"I started back up the river. It was slow going. The river finally froze on me. I got Indians and dog sleds. I was traveling hard and fast, and I went under the name of Bill Hogarty. I told people we'd struck it rich, and that Leeds, my partner, was staying in to watch the claim, that I was going out to get supplies, and bank the gold. I stayed away from people we knew. I did but little talking, and I traveled fast.

"You see, the way I figured it, by traveling as Bill Hogarty, I could leave a record that Bill had left the country and got as far as Seattle. Then in Seattle, I'd take my own name, and talk with people I knew. Then if the law found the body, they wouldn't identify it as Hogarty because the records would show Hogarty had gone out and reached Seattle, where he'd disappeared. They couldn't identify it as Leeds because Leeds would be alive and well. It was the best I could do. I figured that, with any sort of luck, it would be a year or two before they found the body. I got out to Seattle, still going under the name of Hogarty. I found Emily. She'd felt the same way about me I'd felt about her. We were married.

"We lived here in Seattle that winter. We were both of us high-strung and temperamental. We had one hell of a fight in the spring. Emily walked out on me. I know now, she intended to come back, but Emily was as high-strung as a good trotting horse. I left Seattle and went back to my real identity of Alden Leeds."

Leeds stopped talking for a moment, and held a match to his pipe. "Remember," he went on, slowly, "things were different in those days. The country was young, and the men in it were young. Even the old men were younger than most of the young men are now.

"Nowadays, we're suffering from hardening of the economic arteries. The country is old. Our outlook is old. People have quit trying. You could comb through this whole damn city today and not get a half a dozen men with the guts to take what the Yukon dished out in those days. I don't mind getting old and dying. I hate to see the whole damned country dying along with me. There ain't any youth to take our place. Just a bunch of whining little snivelers who want the government to support 'em."

In the silence which followed, knuckles pounded on the door of the room. Mason said, "What is it?"

A bellboy's voice answered, "A telegram for Mr. Mason. He isn't in his room. I thought he might be here. He told the clerk he'd call on Mr. Smith."

"Shove it under the door," Mason said, "and I'll push a dollar bill back. I'm Mason."

A moment later, a blue envelope slid under the door. Mason slid a dollar bill through the crack.

"Okay," Mason said. "I'll let you know if there's an answer."

He ripped open the telegram envelope and read a message sent by Della Street:

OUR OFFICE TELEPHONE LINE AND MY APARTMENT LINE HAVE BEEN TAPPED STOP YOUR CONVERSATION WITH MILTON STIVE OVERHEARD DISTRICT ATTORNEY SERVED SUBPOENA DUCES TECUM DEMANDING ALL PAPERS STOP MY CONVERSATION WITH YOU ABOUT GOING SEATTLE PLANE RESERVATIONS AND LOCATION OF ALDEN LEEDS ALSO APPARENTLY OVERHEARD

DELLA STREET

Mason folded the message, and pushed it down into his coat pocket. He turned back to face the two in the room. "All right," he said quietly, "we're going to have company. You two do exactly as I say. Miss Milicant, here's a key to a room in the hotel. You're registered in that room as Mrs. George L. Manchester. Go to that room. Lock yourself in. Stay there until after the police think you've slipped through their fingers, and have quit watching the place. Then get out, keep under cover, and write me at my office where you are and what name you're using.

"Leeds, I *could* help you escape. I don't think it's wise. When you're arrested, waive extradition, but don't be in a hurry to do it. Tell the police that you're in love with Emily Milicant, that you hope she does you the honor of marrying you, that you had no idea the man you knew as John Milicant was going under the name of Louie Conway until yesterday afternoon. Admit that you called on him, claim that you don't know what time it was; that you had a business matter to discuss; that you

107

left him alive and well; that you won't discuss anything else until after you've talked with Emily. Don't tell the police what you were talking about, what the check was for, or how you found out Conway and Milicant were one and the same.

"Now then, after you left the sanitarium, you wrote out another twenty thousand dollar check also payable to Conway, but endorsed so as to make it payable to bearer. The description of the woman who cashed that check makes me think it was Emily Milicant. How about it?"

They exchanged glances. "It was I," Emily admitted.

"What's the idea?"

"Alden wanted to have plenty of cash to do what he wanted to do. He knew he couldn't draw twenty thousand in cash without making it look as though he were running away. He figured that if he made that second check to Conway and had me cash it, he could get the twenty thousand, and no one would figure he was checking out. It sounded like a good idea at the time."

"It looks like hell now," Mason said. "Twenty grand is too much cash for a pleasure trip. It looks as though you *were* running away and didn't intend to come back."

"I know it," she admitted.

Leeds said, "Look here, Mason, I can't be arrested. I've *got* to get back to the Tanana country."

"Why?"

"Don't you see? To square up that old killing."

"You mean John Milicant was blackmailing you over that?"

"Yes."

"Just what did you expect to do?" Mason asked.

"I expected to go back and clear the thing up."

"How did you expect to square it?" Mason asked.

"I thought I could tell the truth. I thought Emily could back me up."

Mason said, "Don't be foolish. Emily can't back you up. Her story would furnish motivation—that's all. After all this time, the facts are obscured. John had the evidence against you. He
108

gave it to Marcia Whittaker to keep. She gave it to me. I told her you'd stand back of her as long as she kept her mouth shut."

"You have that evidence?" Leeds asked eagerly.

"How about Marcia Whittaker?" Mason asked, avoiding the subject. "Did I do right?"

"Good Heavens, yes! I'd do anything in the world to get that evidence."

Mason turned to Emily Milicant. "How about you?" he asked. "Would you do anything in the world to get Alden out of that old charge?"

She nodded.

Mason frowned thoughtfully. "All right," he said. "Do exactly as I told you, no more and no less. If the police should catch you, refuse to make any statement, refuse to identify the body as that of your brother, refuse to admit you ever had a brother, and refuse to talk about anything until you've seen me. Can you do that?"

"How," she asked, "would that help matters any?"

Mason said, "I haven't time to make explanations. Will you do what I say?"

"Yes."

"If you do exactly that," Mason said, "both of you, I can help you. If you don't follow my instructions, one or both of you is quite apt to get a first degree murder rap pinned on you."

"Your instructions," Leeds said dubiously, "are simple enough, but I don't see how they can help matters. Even if you have all of those papers, there's going to be an investigation. The police will want to know what Conway had on me, why I paid the twenty thousand."

"Don't tell them," Mason said.

"And if I don't tell them, they'll claim I murdered him in order to free myself of a blackmailer."

"Not if I say that he telephoned me after you left," Emily Milicant said.

Leeds stared steadily at her. "You know damn well he didn't telephone you," he said.

Mason said, "Shut up. Now listen to me. Emily, have you any other relatives?"

"No, just the two of us."

Mason said, "John's life must have been a closed book back of a certain date. It must have been, for him to have covered up that felony conviction."

"It was," she said.

Mason said, "Get down to the room where you're Mrs. Manchester. Don't waste any time. After I leave, don't sit here and talk. Don't get sentimental. Don't get excited. Do exactly as I have told you. Remember that the man who killed two birds with one stone had only to throw the rock. We have *one* bird, and we have to account for *two* stones."

He strode out of the room, took the elevator to the lobby. The drizzle had become a cold, steady rain. As Mason stood in the doorway, waiting for a taxicab, a police car rounded a corner and skidded into the curb. Four officers in uniform jumped out. Two plain-clothes men, who had been standing near the door, converged on the group of officers.

Mason's taxicab took him to the telegraph office where he sent Della Street a message, saying simply, "WIRE RECEIVED MAKE NO COMPLAINT ABOUT MATTER MENTIONED DO NOT BE SURPRISED AT ANY CONVERSATIONS I HAVE WITH YOU OVER TELEPHONE."

He signed the wire, paid for it, returned to his taxi, and said, "Take me to a newspaper office. I want to put an ad in the personal column."

At the newspaper office, Mason, with moisture glistening on his suit and dripping from the brim of his hat, wrote an ad for the personals. "Wanted: Information concerning the past life of William Hogarty, age fifty-four years, walks with slight limp because four toes of right features, partially bald, black eyes, black hair. In 1906, Height, five feet ten. Weight, a hundred and eighty. Heavy features, partially bald, black eyes, black hair. In 1906, Hogarty went to Tanana district to Klondike. Returned Seattle sometime in 1907. Has gone under name of L. C. Conway. Any accurate information as to past life, heirs and

110

former associates of this man will receive liberal reward. Particularly anxious to find doctor who performed operation on frostbitten foot and learn what, if any, statements were made by Hogarty at that time. Communicate Perry M. care this paper."

Mason shoved the ad across the counter. "Here," he said, "is a fifty-dollar bill. Keep this ad running until the money's used up or until I tell you to stop. Run it in display type, or double-space it, or whatever is necessary to attract attention."

"Yes, sir," the girl said, looking at his wet clothes. "It must be raining outside."

Mason shivered, passed one of his cards across the counter. "Any replies you receive," he said, "are to be sent at once by air-mail to this address. Do you understand?"

"Yes, sir."

"Good night," Mason said, and strode out into the cold rain. "If I can't buy an overcoat, " he told the cab driver, "perhaps I can find an airplane that will carry me far enough south to get into a different climate."

The cab driver looked at him in amazement.

"In other words," Mason said, "the airport, and make it snappy."

At the airport, Mason found that the next regular passenger plane left Seattle at ten-thirty-five the next morning. The taxicab took him to one of the city's better hotels where he again registered and explained to the clerk that he had no baggage.

In his room, Mason enjoyed the luxury of a hot bath and a night's sleep. In the morning, he called Della Street on the long distance telephone. "Get my message?" he asked.

"Yes."

Mason said, "Listen, Della. Here are the developments. I located Alden Leeds up here. I've found out quite a bit of family history. John Milicant was Leeds' former partner. He went by the name of Bill Hogarty. He and Leeds went into the Klondike in 1906. They struck it rich. Hogarty and Leeds had a falling out over a dance hall girl. The dance hall girl was Emily Milicant. Hogarty married Emily Milicant in Seattle in 1907."

111

"Then he wasn't Emily Milicant's brother?"

"Not a bit of it," Mason said.

"But why did she say he was?"

"It's a long story," Mason said. "I think we can identify the body absolutely as that of Hogarty because of his frostbitten foot. But we want to keep the district attorney from finding out what we're doing."

Della Street said, "Is there anything you want me to do at this end, Chief?"

Mason said, "Yes. Explain to Phyllis Leeds that everything is okay, and that I'll be back in the office Monday morning. Tell her I've seen her uncle; that he's all right and wants to be remembered to her."

"Where," Della Street asked, "is her uncle now?"

Mason said, "The last I saw of him he was at his hotel."

"Are you in the same hotel?"

"No. I registered again in a second hotel because I didn't want Leeds to be interrupting me with a lot of questions. I was tired and wanted to sleep. See you tomorrow, Della. 'By."

Mason hung up, went down to the lobby, paid his bill, and caught the plane south. It was still raining.

In San Francisco, Mason bought a newspaper. He found what he wanted on the second page. While he was flying to Los Angeles, he read the newspaper account with twinkling eyes:

KLONDIKE MILLIONAIRE WANTED FOR MURDERING SAME MAN IN TWO STATES. KNOTTY EXTRADITION PROBLEM PRESENTED TO WASHINGTON GOVERNOR.

Seattle, Washington. Did Alden Leeds murder Bill Hogarty in the Klondike in 1906? Did Bill Hogarty murder Alden Leeds in the Klondike in 1906? Or did Alden Leeds murder William Hogarty in California last Friday night?

These are questions which are perplexing the authorities and causing a particular headache to the Governor of the State of Washington, who is advised that he will shortly receive, in due form, demands that Alden Leeds, who is at present held a prisoner in Seattle, be returned to Alaskan authorities to answer to the charge of murdering Bill Hogarty, his mining partner, back in the later days of the Klondike gold rush. On the other hand, California authorities, who have appeared on the ground in Seattle, are equally positive that Alden Leeds murdered Bill Hogarty no later than last Friday night.

A discrepancy of thirty-three years in the date of a man's demise is startling, to say the least, to say nothing of the fact that it is virtually an impossibility for a man to be murdered in Alaska and then again in California. There is, in the popular mind, a supposition that murder is a final gesture. The corpse is supposed to remain in, what the lawyers term, *status quo*.

Alaskan authorities claim that they have found the body of Bill Hogarty where it was left in a shallow grave by Alden Leeds following a rich strike which the partners made in a mining claim. The Alaskan authorities claim to have evidence showing that Leeds disguised his identity by taking none other than the name of the murdered man, and left the Yukon, masquerading as Bill Hogarty. So completely were the officers fooled by this clever ruse, that for years they were searching for Bill Hogarty, on the theory that he had murdered Alden Leeds.

California authorities, however, claim that the Alaskan body was not that of Bill Hogarty because Bill Hogarty was killed by Alden Leeds no later than last Friday night, and cite a frostbitten foot on the part of the corpse to prove identity.

The situation is rendered more puzzling in view of the fact that a well-known criminal attorney, whose dramatic exploits have attracted more than state-wide attention, has instituted a frantic search for information concerning the deceased Bill Hogarty, and, in particular, as to the manner in which he lost his toes.

To the layman, the whole affair appears puzzling, to say the least. It is as though Alden Leeds, having murdered Bill

113

Hogarty in the Klondike in 1906, was subsequently confronted with the body of a corpse which had refused to accept the murder as final, and who had suffered only the amputation of four toes from his right foot as the result of thirty-three years' interment in an icy grave in the far north. Whereupon, as though to illustrate the maxim of, if at first you don't succeed, try, try again, the dead man was murdered again—so that now all that is mortal of Bill Hogarty lies in a Southern California mortuary undoubtedly quite dead, frostbitten foot and all.

It is to be borne in mind that the contention of the authorities that Alden Leeds is the murderer is as yet entirely unsubstantiated in any court of justice. It is quite possible that Alden Leeds could make a statement which would go far toward explaining the matter, but Alden Leeds has become afflicted with a temporary impediment of speech which prevents him from answering any questions.

Emily Milicant, whom the authorities insist was occupying a room with Alden Leeds in Seattle, has also mysteriously vanished. Inasmuch as she seemed to evaporate into thin air during a time when the hotel was under the closest surveillance, the authorities are, to put the matter mildly, irritated. They insist that there is more than a casual coincidence in the fact that Miss Milicant's astounding disappearance into the Seattle atmosphere coincide with the arrival on the scene of a noted criminal lawyer.

Della Street and Paul Drake were waiting for Mason at the airport. "Hello, gang," Mason said. "How about eats?"

"Swell," Della Street said. "There's a fine restaurant right here in the main administration building."

Mason said, "And we won't discuss any business until after we've finished with the food."

On the way to the restaurant, Drake said, "Seen the papers about Leeds, Perry?"

"Uh huh."

"Where," Drake asked, "did you get that dope about the frostbitten foot?"

Mason said firmly, "We eat now and talk later."

Drake said, "I always like to eat with a client who's on an expense account."

Mason grinned. "Go as far as you like."

"I take it then," Drake said, "Leeds was appreciative—and generous."

"And I'll discuss *that* over the coffee and cigarettes," Mason said.

When they had finished the meal and were huddled over cups of black coffee, Mason lit a cigarette and said to Paul Drake, "Okay, Paul, let's have it."

Drake said, "Following your tip-off, Della had me check on the tenants above the sixth floor in that apartment house. We drew blanks until we looked up the occupant of 881. She's Inez Colton—has a secretarial job in a hardware store. She's been seen two or three times with a young man who drove a red convertible. Jason Carrel has a red convertible. Descriptions on the cars check absolutely. What's more, Inez Colton took a powder right after the murder. We can't locate her anywhere. She simply walked out and disappeared. She told a friend she was going on a week-end trip."

Mason said, "Jason Carrel, eh? It sounds as though we've struck pay dirt, Paul."

"Struck it," Drake said, "but can't do anything with it. We've got men covering Jason Carrel. He *may* lead us to her, but I think he's too wise.

"The officers slapped a subpoena *duces tecum* on your handwriting expert. That meant either that Della had been shadowed when she went to him, or that the telephone line was tapped. I did a little investigating and found out your telephone line to the office and hers at her apartment were tapped."

"How about this waitress at the Home Kitchen Cafe?" Mason asked.

"I don't think there's anything to that," Drake said.

115

"She left before the murder was committed. Evidently, it's just a coincidence."

"What time did she leave?"

"Around nine o'clock. Someone saw her leaving her room. She was carrying two heavy suitcases. I tried to cover taxicabs, but can't find anything as yet. Her room rent was paid up. She had wages coming. Oscar Baker is the waiter at the Blue and White Restaurant who took the dinner up. He's positive on the time element. He doesn't know Hazel Stickland, the waitress at the Home Kitchen Cafe—says he doesn't, and I'm inclined to believe him, but I'm checking back on him. He's just a punk kid who's drifted around, flunky in a lumber camp, waiter, dishwasher—plays what money he can get on the horses—a colorless chap who's never found himself because there isn't anything to find. I've planted an operative who's become friendly with him, posing as a waiter out of a job. Baker says he'll try and get him on at the Blue and White as soon as there's a vacancy."

Mason said, "You can't tell about kids these days, Paul. A lot of the most puzzling crimes and the most vicious crimes are committed by persons under twenty-five."

"I know," Drake said, "and, of course, there's a possible motivation. John Milicant was quite a ladies' man. He played the races. Hazel played the races, and Oscar Baker played them. But that doesn't mean anything. A lot of people play the ponies these days.

"I find that Oscar Baker has been winning money crap shooting lately and losing it on ponies. From the way he's been winning with craps, I wouldn't doubt that he had some of the merchandise of the Conway Appliance Company."

"Check on that?" Mason asked.

"Hell," Drake said, "he's too wise. My operative got in a crap game with him, and won three dollars. If Baker had any crooked dice from Conway, he was wise enough to ditch them as soon as he read about the murder.

"Serle has sold us outright. Naturally, you'd have to expect that. *I* think that he talked with Conway at ten-thirty, but he's

116

fixed the time at ten o'clock now. Of course, there wasn't any bribery or anything like that, but, as one of the main witnesses for the prosecution, the D.A. wouldn't want him to come into court as a crook. So they're covering him with a thick coat of whitewash; and, of course, Serle was smart enough to figure that all out. He didn't have to be awfully smart to do that.

"Incidentally, while we're checking up on things, don't overlook this prospector friend of Leeds—Ned Barkler."

"What about him?" Mason asked.

"He's a card," Drake said, "talks occasionally about the old days in the Yukon country, never mentions any of his own adventures, becomes interested in stories of frontier brawls, and shooting scrapes. For the most part, he wears disreputable clothes, but occasionally he spruces himself up and steps out. He looks the girls over with an appraising eye, and makes passes at the pretty ones when he thinks he can get away with it—cashiers in restaurants, girls at cigar counter, manicurists, and janes like that."

"Successful?" Mason asked.

"Hell, Perry," the detective protested. "Give me a chance. I haven't even located him yet. He's a colorful profane old coot who's as salty as a piece of smoked salmon. But where the devil he came from before he contacted Leeds, is more than I can find out. He appeared a couple of years ago, right in the middle of the picture. And now that he's left, he's walked right out of the middle of the picture. Somehow, Perry, I have an idea there's one man we'll never find until he wants us to find him."

Mason said, "I want Inez Colton, Paul, and I want her badly."

"How much time can I have?" Drake asked.

"None at all," Mason said. "I'm going to rush that preliminary hearing through just as fast as I can."

"Why not stall along until I can turn up something on the Colton woman?"

Mason shook his head. "Don't forget the D.A. has served a subpoena *duces tecum* on my handwriting expert. I want to mix this case up so much and rush it through so fast that he'll be one jump behind us all the way along the line. When he sees those

117

papers, I don't want him to have time enough to figure out what they mean."

"It'll take work and luck," Drake said. "I'll furnish the work. You'll have to pray for luck. What's all this about Milicant being Hogarty, Perry, and how did you find out about that frost-bitten foot?"

Mason smiled at Della Street. "A little bird told me," he said.

Chapter 11

Judge Knox, who had acquired a great respect for Perry Mason's courtroom technique, by presiding over the preliminary hearing in what the press had subsequently referred to as "The Case of the Stuttering Bishop," gazed down on the crowded courtroom, and said, "Gentlemen, in the Case of the People of the State of California versus Alden Leeds, accused of the murder of John Milicant, sometimes known as Bill Hogarty, also referred to as L. C. Conway, the defendant has previously been advised of his constitutional rights. This is the time heretofore fixed pursuant to stipulation for the preliminary hearing. Are you ready?"

Bob Kittering, of the district attorney's office, a thin, nervous individual with restless eyes, answered, "Ready on behalf of the People, Your Honor."

"Ready for the defendant," Mason said.

"Proceed," Judge Knox instructed.

The deputy coroner was the first witness. He testified at length concerning the finding of the body, introduced photographs showing its position on the floor of the bathroom, showing the fatal knife which protruded from the back, just above the left shoulder blade. He also produced photographs showing the state of the apartment with the evidences of hasty search. Under further questioning by Kittering, he produced an envelope which contained the personal possessions of the decedent which had been taken from the pockets of his clothes.

Kittering said, "I observe that there is a fountain pen, a handkerchief, a jackknife, six dollars and twelve cents in loose change found in the trousers pocket of the deceased, an envelope with no return address, addressed to L. C. Conway, and

119

containing scribbled memoranda. There is a pigskin key container, a watch, a cigarette case, and a pocket lighter. I call your attention to the fact that there is no wallet, no driving license, no business cards, and no currency, and ask you if you are absolutely certain that these items and these items alone were all that you found in the clothes of the deceased."

"That is correct," the deputy coroner said.

"No wallet was found in the clothing, and none was subsequently found in the apartment?"

"So far as I know, that is correct. No wallet was ever discovered."

"Take the witness," Kittering said.

"No cross-examination," Mason announced urbanely.

The autopsy surgeon was called and testified at some length. He commented on the fact that from the state of the body, as he had discovered it, death had been caused by a downward thrust of a long-handled carving-knife which was still imbedded in the wound. This instrument had been inserted on a downward slope, clearing the left shoulder blade and penetrating the heart. Death, in his opinion, had been instantaneous. The time of death he fixed as approximately from eight to fourteen hours prior to the time he had made his examination.

Kittering produced a bloodstained carving knife. "I call your attention to this knife, Doctor, and ask you if this is the knife which you found imbedded in the body of the decedent?"

"It is," the doctor said.

Kittering asked that the knife be marked for identification as People's Exhibit A.

"No objection," Mason drawled.

"Can you," Kittering asked, "fix the time of death any more definitely than that, Doctor?"

"Not in relation to the time when I examined the body, but I can fix it *very* definitely in regard to the contents of the stomach."

"What do you mean, Doctor?"

"I mean that in examining the contents of the stomach, and submitting them to an examination for the purposes of de-

120

tecting the possible presence of poison, we found that the person in question had died approximately two hours after a meal consisting primarily of mutton, probably in the form of chops, green peas, and potatoes, had been consumed. . . . In order to explain my answer, I may state that while the time of death as fixed in postmortem depends upon various elastic factors such as *rigor mortis*, the cooling of the body, etc., and is, therefore, subject to a certain amount of individual variation, the processes of digestion are more uniform; and by examining the state to which those digestive processes have progressed prior to death, we can, when there is food in the stomach, fix the time of death with much greater nicety."

"Can you," Kittering asked, "fix the exact time of death?"

"In view of the evidence," the doctor said positively, "I fix the time of death definitely as not before ten o'clock in the evening preceding that of the day in which the body was discovered and not later then ten-forty-five on the evening of said day."

"How do you fix that time?" Kittering asked.

"By an examination of the extent to which the digestive processes had functioned, in connection with the time at which the last meal had been consumed."

Kittering said triumphantly, "You may inquire."

Mason said to the court, "Of course, Your Honor, I could move to strike out this entire testimony on the theory that it is predicated upon facts which are beyond the doctor's knowledge."

"This testimony will be connected up," Kittering said.

"Well," Mason observed, "to save time, I won't make the motion, but to get the record clear, I'll ask a few questions. . . . How do you determine the time of death when you are performing a post-mortem, Doctor?"

"Under circumstances such as this," the doctor said, with acid hostility, "there are various methods. An examination of the stomach content where there is food in the stomach and data available as to the time of ingestion is by far the best method."

"Acting," Mason said, "on the assumption that dinner was served and eaten at eight-ten?"

"Acting on the assumption that dinner was served at eight-ten. Yes, sir."

"But," Mason pointed out, "your only knowledge of when dinner was eaten is predicated entirely upon what has been told you. Isn't that right?"

The doctor raised his voice. "There are witnesses to prove it."

"If it should turn out the wtinesses are mistaken in their time, then you are mistaken in your time. Is that right?"

"The witness isn't mistaken," the doctor said. "I've talked with him personally."

"But all you know of your own knowledge, Doctor, is that you performed an autopsy on a body, that death had occurred from eight to fourteen hours prior to the time you made your examination and within approximately two hours of the time the deceased partook of a meal consisting of certain specific articles of food?"

"You can put it that way if you want to," the doctor snapped.

"Thank you, Doctor," Mason said with a smile. "I want to. That's all. You're excused."

"Jason Carrel will be the next witness," Kittering announced.

Carrel, poker-faced, steady-eyed, came forward, raised his right hand, and was sworn. He gave his name and residence. "Did you," Kittering asked, "see a body at the funeral parlors of Breckenbridge & Manifred?"

"I did."

"When was that?"

"On the morning of Saturday, the seventh."

"And did you identify that body?"

"I did."

"Had you been acquainted with that man during his lifetime?"

"Yes."

"Under what name did you know him?"

"Under the name of John Milicant, a brother of Emily Milicant."

122

"And do you know whether this defendant, Alden Leeds, your uncle, also knew the deceased?"

"Yes, he did."

"Under what name?"

"Objected to as calling for a conclusion of the witness," Mason said. "He can't testify as to what his uncle knows."

"Sustained."

"Did you ever hear your uncle call him by name?"

"I did."

"Under what name did your uncle address him?" Kittering asked triumphantly.

"As John Milicant."

"You may inquire," Kittering said.

"You have no particular affection for your uncle, the defendant in this case?" Mason inquired conversationally.

"On the contrary, I really care for him," Carrel retorted. "I care enough for him so that I realized he was in danger of being victimized by an unscrupulous adventuress, and took steps to prevent him being stripped of his property."

"And by the unscrupulous adventuress, you refer to Emily Milicant, the sister of the deceased?"

"I do."

"Now then," Mason said conversationally, "suppose that it should appear that the defendant in this case was not your uncle. Would that make any difference in connection with your testimony?"

"What do you mean?"

"Simply this. Suppose that in the event of his death—either by natural causes or in the gas chamber at San Quentin—you stood no chance of profiting, in other words, that you were not a natural heir of his and, therefore, not in a position to share in his estate or contest his will, would you continue your efforts to prevent his marriage or regard the possibility that he might be convicted of murder with equal satisfaction?"

Kittering jumped to his feet. "Your Honor," he shouted. "Your Honor, this is outrageous! This is uncalled for. This is unethical and unprofessional. It is quite on a par with the tactics that counsel has used in . . . "

Judge Knox interrupted calmly to say, "The question is not temperate. It may not be considerate. Doubtless, it is not courteous, but it is legal. I know of no law which requires counsel to be courteous, temperate, or considerate with witnesses who testify adversely. The question goes to show motivation, bias, and a possible reason. Therefore, it will be allowed."

"Answer the question," Mason said.

"I care nothing whatever about my uncle's money," Carrel said in a low voice.

"But you did have him strong-armed out of an automobile in order to place him in an institution when you thought he was about to marry Emily Milicant."

"I did that for his own good."

"And your own good, your own advantage, didn't enter into the matter at all?" Mason asked suavely.

Carrel hesitated a minute, fidgeted uneasily, then raised sullen eyes, and said, "No."

"And you didn't discuss with the other two relatives who cooperated with you in that action, the advisability of having your uncle committed to an institution so that you could prevent his marriage, prevent his making a valid will, and thereby insure your participation in the fruits of his lifelong savings?"

Carrel again fidgeted, and then said without looking up, "No."

"There was no conversation to that effect?"

"No."

"The matter wasn't mentioned in your presence by any of the others?"

Again there was a long silence. Again Carrel answered without looking up, "No."

"Your action in kidnaping your uncle was actuated by the loftiest motives and without any thought whatever for your own financial interest?"

"Objected to," Kittering snapped. "Assuming facts not in evidence. I object particularly to the use of the word 'kidnaping.' "

"Sustained," Judge Knox said.

Mason smiled. "You have admitted that you attempted to have your uncle declared incompetent and placed in an institution?"

As the witness hesitated, Mason opened his brief case, and said, "I have here a copy of your sworn statement if you wish to refresh your recollection, Mr. Carrel."

"Yes," Carrel said, "I did."

"And you tricked him into entering the grounds of an institution where two male nurses, at your request, forcibly dragged him from an automobile and detained him against his will?"

"It wasn't at my request."

"Oh, you had nothing to do with that?"

"No."

"You asked Dr. Parkin C. Londonberry to have that done, didn't you?"

"I asked him to give my uncle proper treatment."

"And explained to him that by proper treatment, you meant that your uncle should be confined?"

"Well, yes—in a way."

"Now, are you acquainted with an Inez Colton?"

"No," Jason Carrel shouted.

"You don't know her?"

"No."

"Have never met her?"

"No."

"Do you know anyone who lives in the apartment house where this decedent resided and where his body was found?"

"No."

Mason regarded him with narrowed eyes. "You're aware that you're under oath, and that this is a murder case?"

"Naturally."

"And your answers still stand?"

"Yes."

"That," Mason announced, "is all."

Judge Knox, in a manner which plainly showed his complete disbelief, said, "Mr. Carrel, do you wish this court to understand that during the time you and your relatives were discussing the steps you were taking to have your uncle, the defendant in this case, declared incompetent, there was never at any time in your presence any conversation whatever as to the material advantages which would result in behalf of any of the relatives from preventing your uncle's marriage, preventing him from making a valid will, or prevailing in your action to have him declared incompetent?"

Carrel shifted his eyes, looked at Mason for a moment, then turned appealingly to Kittering. In an almost inaudible voice, he said, "There was never any such conversation."

"That's all," Judge Knox said, his voice as ominously final as the closing of a steel trap.

Kittering seemed uneasy. "Of course, Mr. Carrel," he said, "I take it that you might have *casually* mentioned that you were your uncle's heirs, and were safeguarding his fortune for him."

"Objected to as leading and suggestive," Mason said.

"Objection sustained," Judge Knox said.

Kittering said, "Well, did you discuss indirectly any financial benefit which might have occurred to you?"

"No," Carrel said.

"Witness excused," Kittering announced, his voice showing his impatience. "I will call Freeman Leeds to the stand."

Freeman Leeds, a big, powerful man, whose face had set with age into lines of sullen defiance, took the oath, gave his name and address to the reporter, and took the witness stand.

"You are a brother of the defendant in this case?"

"Yes."

"Have you at any time discussed with the defendant a person known as Bill Hogarty?"

"Yes."

"When?"

"Upon two or three occasions. I can't remember the exact dates."

"And what did the defendant say about Hogarty?"

"Objected to," Mason said, "as incompetent, irrelevant, and immaterial."

"I offer to connect it up," Kittering said.

126

"On that understanding, the objection will be overruled," Judge Knox said.

Freeman Leeds said, "Alden had been up in the Klondike. He told me something about his adventures up there. He'd struck it rich, and Bill Hogarty had been his partner on the claim when they struck it rich."

"Did the defendant describe William Hogarty to you in any way?"

"He said Hogarty was younger than he was, but a strong lad," Freeman Leeds said.

"Did he make any further statements about Hogarty?"

"Said Hogarty and he had some trouble."

"Did he say what the trouble was?"

"I understood it was over a woman."

"Not what you understood," Kittering corrected. "Did he specifically say that?"

"Yes, he said it was over a dance hall girl."

"Did he say anything more about the trouble?"

"At one time, he said that he'd been in a shooting scrape over a woman."

"Did he say where that shooting occurred?"

"Up in the Klondike some place."

"You may cross-examine," Kittering said.

"May I ask," Mason inquired, "the object of this examination? Is it the contention of the prosecution that this vague testimony goes to show that the body is that of Bill Hogarty?"

"That is our contention," Kittering said. "Your Honor, we expect to connect this up. We expect to introduce evidence tending to show that this defendant forged the name of Bill Hogarty to various hotel registers, that when he left the Klondike he went for a time under the name of Bill Hogarty; that he took with him all of Bill Hogarty's share in the mining claim, that this decedent is none other than Bill Hogarty, that Hogarty attempted to secure some financial adjustment from the defendant, and the defendant, rather than part with any of his fraudulent gains, planned to murder Hogarty. In that way, we expect to show motivation for the crime."

127

"You have all of the proof necessary to show that?" Mason inquired blandly.

"We have all we need," Kittering snapped. "Some of it we will prove by inference, but you don't need to appear so surprised, Mr. Mason. Your ad in the personal columns of the Seattle paper shows that you . . ."

"That will do," Judge Knox interrupted. "Counsel will refrain from personalities. You will proceed with cross-examination of the witness, Mr. Mason."

Mason said, "Very well, Your Honor. Now, Mr. Leeds, I am going to ask you the same question that I asked Jason Carrel. Was there any conversation which took place in your presence or in the presence of Jason Carrel to the effect that it would be to your financial advantage, either directly or indirectly, to have Alden Leeds declared incompetent or committed to an institution?"

Leeds took a deep breath. "I'd rather not answer that question."

"Go ahead and answer it," Mason said.

"It's a proper question," Judge Knox ruled.

"Your Honor," Kittering objected desperately, "if counsel wishes to impeach Jason Carrel, he must do it as a part of his own case, not by trying to force one of my witnesses into making the impeachment."

"I don't agree with you," Judge Knox said. "This question goes to show bias on the part of this witness. It is quite obvious that if the defendant is convicted of a crime it will prevent the consummation of a marriage which apparently is and was objectionable to his relatives. You may answer the question, Mr. Leeds."

"There was some talk about my being appointed guardian."

"Any talk about any financial advantage to accrue from that appointment?"

Freeman Leeds became silent for several uneasy seconds. "No," he said at length.

"And no talk about the possibility of any of you inheriting a part of the defendant's fortune?"

Leeds hesitated. "No," he said.

128

"The defendant is your older brother?"

"Yes."

"How old were you when the defendant left home?"

"I was seven years old."

"When did you next see him again?"

"About five years ago."

"And you had no contact with him in the meantime?"

"No."

"You didn't hear from him?"

"No."

"Didn't know where he was?"

"No."

"How did you know this defendant is your brother?"

"I recognized him," Leeds said.

Mason smiled. "Would you," he asked suavely, "have recognized him if he had been broke?"

A ripple of laughter swept the courtroom, swelled in one or two instances into a guffaw of mirth. Judge Knox, fighting to keep a smile from his lips, said, "The court will come to order. We'll have no more laughter. The question is adroitly framed, conveying as it does, an entire argument by inference. However, the spectators will cease from giving any expressions of amusement or interrupting the order of proceedings. Answer the question, Mr. Leeds."

Freeman Leeds said, "Of course, I'd have recognized him."

"And if he'd appeared at your back door with a roll of blankets over his shoulder, ragged, unkempt, and asking for a meal, do you think you would have forthwith recognized him as your long-lost brother?"

"Yes."

"Where did the meeting take place, Mr. Leeds?"

"Alden Leeds drove up to my house."

"In a taxicab?"

"Yes."

"And what did he say?"

"He asked me if I didn't remember him, and if I couldn't

129

place him. Then, after a while, he said, 'Don't you remember your own brother, Alden Leeds?' "

"I see," Mason said with a smile. "There was some interval between the time when he asked if you didn't know him and couldn't place him?"

"Yes."

"How long?"

"A minute or two."

"And during all of that time, you failed to recognize him?"

"Well, I wasn't exactly sure."

"I see. And after Alden Leeds made the announcement, did you then recognize him?"

"Well, I told him to come in."

"And the defendant entered your house?"

"Yes."

"And talked for some time?"

"For an hour or so, yes."

"And at that time, he told you that he had made a fortune in the Klondike?"

"Well, he said he was pretty well fixed."

"And," Mason said, "after he had made that statement, your recognition of him as your brother became positive, did it not?"

Leeds said, "That isn't fair."

"Why isn't it fair?"

"I recognized him."

"When?"

"As soon as I saw him."

"Before he had entered the house?"

"Yes, of course."

"But you didn't call him by name, and you couldn't place him during the time he was waiting for you to place him?"

"Well, not exactly."

"And did you shake hands with him?"

"I don't remember."

"Was anyone else present at the conversation?"

"During the last part of it, yes."

"And who was that?"

"Jason Carrel."

"And did you introduce the defendant to Jason Carrel?"

"Yes, I did."

"Do you remember exactly what you said?"

"That's been five or six years ago," the witness protested. "It's hard to remember things over that length of time."

"Not for a man with your remarkable memory," Mason said. "I believe you stated your age was sixty-five. You were, therefore, about sixty when you saw your brother. You had last seen him when you were seven years old, and yet you recognized him instantly over this lapse of fifty-three years. Isn't that right?"

"Well . . . Well, yes."

"Now specifically what did you say to Jason Carrel? Did you say, 'Jason, this is my brother, Alden'?"

"Well, I can't remember."

"As a matter of fact, " Mason said, "didn't you say words to this effect, 'Jason, this man claims to be your Uncle Alden.' "

"Well, something like that."

Mason smiled. "That is all," he said.

Kittering frowned. "My next witness," he said, "is Oscar Baker. . . . The court will pardon me. I am not proving the *corpus delicti* in the regularly accepted order. Some of these witnesses have asked to be excused, and it will be necessary for me to connect some of these things up later."

"You will have an opportunity to connect up your evidence," Judge Knox said. "The court wishes to hear the fullest proof."

"Oscar Baker," Kittering said.

A sallow-skinned lad in the early twenties, whose clothes were the cheapest of ready-mades, yet cut in most extreme style, pinch-waisted his way across the courtroom, held up his hand, and was sworn. He gave his name as Oscar Baker, his occupation as a waiter, his age as twenty-three, his residence as in a rooming house.

"Where are you working?" Kittering asked.

"At the Blue and White Restaurant."

"You are employed as a waiter there?"

"Yes."

"How long have you been so employed?"

"I've been there going on to six months," Baker said.

"And you were so employed there as a waiter on the evening of the seventh of this month?"

"I was."

"That was a Friday evening, I believe?"

"Yes, sir."

"What time did you go to work?"

"At four o'clock in the afternoon."

"At what time did you get off?"

"At eleven o'clock at night."

"Were you acquainted with a John Milicant?"

"I was, yes, sir."

"Had you seen him on several occasions?"

"Yes, sir."

"Where?"

"At his apartment house. It's only a half a block down the street from the restaurant."

"And what were the occasions on which you had seen him?"

"When I brought meals up to him."

"He occasionally ordered meals in his apartment?"

"Yes."

"These meals were ordered from your restaurant, and you took them up in the course of your employment as a waiter?"

"Yes, sir. That's right."

"Now, on the evening in question, did you so serve a meal?"

"Yes, sir. I did."

"How was that order received?"

"Over the telephone."

"Who ordered it?"

"Why, Mr. Milicant, I suppose."

"What did he order?"

"He said he wanted dinner for two. He said he was very particular to get some mutton chops, peas and potatoes. He said to send out for the chops if I had to, but he wanted chops."

"When was that order received?"

"At five minutes to eight."

"How did you happen to notice the time?"

"Because I told him it might take a little time to get the mutton chops. I wasn't certain we had any."

"Did you have some?"

"Yes. When I went back to talk with the cook, I found out we did, although they weren't on the bill of fare that night. He just had a few in the icebox, not enough to put on the menu, but he made up an order for two all right."

"And you took this meal to the apartment?"

"I did."

"That was John Milicant's apartment?"

"Yes, sir."

"Now just explain to the court what happened when you took the food up there."

"Well, I put the dishes on a tray, covered the tray with napkins and a folded tablecloth, and went into the apartment house. I knew the number of Milicant's apartment—Conway, we called him."

"That's L. C. Conway?" Kittering interrupted.

"Yeah, Louie Conway. Well, I took the food up in the elevator, and knocked on the door. A voice yelled, 'Come in.' I opened the door and went in."

"The door was unlocked?" Kittering interjected.

"That's right, and the two guys—I mean men—were in the bedroom. I could hear them talking in there something about race horses, and I sort of kept my ears peeled because Louie Conway sometimes had some pretty good tips on race horses.

"Well, nothing came of it. I think they knew I was listening because the other guy said, 'Wait a minute. The boy's out there.' And then he popped his head out the door, and said, 'Just put it there on the table, son, and come back when we call you and pick up the dishes. How much is the check?' And I said, 'One-seventy-five.' He handed me three one-dollar bills, and said, 'That'll pay you for coming up. Now beat it.'

" 'Want me to set the table?' " I asked.

" 'No,' he said, 'we're in a rush.'

133

" 'That food should be eaten right away,' I told him. 'I heated up the dishes before I left, but carrying it out in the air ain't helped it none.' And this guy said, 'Yeah, I know. On your way, son. We're busy.' "

"Did you know that man?" Kittering asked.

"I didn't then. I do now. It was Guy Serle, the man that bought out Conway's business."

"You know about Conway's business?" Kittering asked.

"Uh huh."

"What kind of business was it?"

"Objected to as incompetent, irrelevant, and immaterial," Mason said.

Judge Knox inquired of Kittering, "Is this for the purpose of showing the real identity of the murdered man, counselor?"

"Well, not exactly," Kittering said, "but for the general purpose of showing the man's background and . . . "

"Objection sustained," Judge Knox said. "You can introduce evidence tending to prove the man's identity. You have now introduced proof that the decedent was John Milicant, that he was also known as L. C. Conway, or Louie Conway. There has been some evidence concerning a Bill Hogarty, but so far there has been no evidence definitely establishing that the decedent and Bill Hogarty were one and the same. The court will give you every latitude in the matter, Mr. Deputy District Attorney, but in the face of objection, where there is no question of proving motive, malice, or opportunity by that line of interrogation, the court will not permit a collateral examination into the business affairs of the decedent. That, of course, is a general ruling. It may well be that, as your case opens up, the evidence will become pertinent. If you wish to connect it up, the court will receive it on your statement that it will be connected up and that it relates to some particular aspect of the case which it is incumbent upon the state to prove."

"We'll not try to connect it up for the present," Kittering said, scowling across at Perry Mason.

"Very well, the objection is well taken and is sustained."

"Did you go back for the dishes?" Kittering asked.

"Yes, that's right. I went back about quarter of an hour before I was scheduled to go off duty."

"That would be ten-forty-five."

"Just about. They hadn't called, so I went back."

"And what did you find?"

"The door was slightly open. I don't know who was in the bedroom. The door was closed. My dishes were empty and stacked on the tray. There was nothing for me to hesitate over. I'd had my tip, and, gosh, I don't know . . . I had an idea maybe there was a jane in there. Well, you know what I mean—well, anyway, that he didn't want to be disturbed."

"Do you *know* whether anyone was in the bedroom?"

"I think so, yeah. I think I heard someone in there. There was a jane's handkerchief—I mean a woman's handkerchief on the side of the table right by the napkin."

"How do you know it was a woman's handkerchief?" Kittering asked.

"I smelled it," Baker announced, and once more a ripple of merriment ran across the courtroom.

"So what did you do?"

"I took the tray with the dishes, and beat it."

"Did you lock the door behind you?"

"I pulled it shut. I think the spring lock was caught back so that the door didn't lock, but I ain't absolutely certain about that. I know I closed the door. If they didn't want it locked, that was their business. If they did, they could lock it."

"Now, are you certain as to the time?"

"Absolutely. We've got an electric clock down there, and I figured Conway—Milicant—might get sore if I didn't get the grub up to him in time. So I noticed particularly the time when the order came in, and kept hurrying the cook up to get it out. You know, in a joint like that—I mean in a restaurant of that size—a waiter can't take food out until he catches a slack time. We really ain't equipped to handle much room service like that. The cook gets the stuff going, and then, in case you're rushed, he keeps it in the hot oven until you get a chance to break away. That keeps the dishes hot, and the food hot. And you'd be surprised how much difference a hot dish makes, particularly when you cover it with a napkin and tablecloth."

"And what time did you return for the dishes?"

"Almost exactly quarter 'til eleven. I'd waited for a slack time—maybe sort of put it off. Then I almost forgot 'em. It was fifteen minutes before my quitting time, so I beat it up there fast."

"And you are positive as to the time you delivered the food?"

"Absolutely. I left right around eight minutes past eight. I got up there at eight-ten on the dot. I'll bet that doesn't miss it ten seconds either way."

"And this was an electric clock in the restaurant?"

"Yes."

"Cross-examine." Kittering tossed the remark across to Perry Mason as though daring him to try to rattle this witness.

"Those electric clocks are always right?" Mason asked.

"Sure, that's why they put them in."

"Except when the power is temporarily interrupted?"

"Well, that sometimes happens," the young man admitted.

"In this instance, how do you know that there hadn't been a temporary interruption in power?"

"There's a place on the clock that shows a signal when that happens."

"And did you notice that place particularly?"

"Well, not particularly, but . . . Shucks, if it had been anything to notice, I'd have noticed it. I always go by that in telling the time."

"But nevertheless you *may* have been mistaken?"

"Not one chance in ten thousand."

"Then there *is* one chance in ten thousand that you were mistaken?" Mason asked.

"Well, if you want to play a ten thousand to one shot," Baker said, "you're welcome to. I don't. Twenty to one is my limit."

Again the courtroom stirred with a comment of whisper and suppressed laughter.

"Now when you returned to get these dishes, no one said anything to you?"

136

"No, sir."

"You gathered the impression there were people in the bedroom?"

"Uh huh."

"Did you think one of those persons was Serle?"

"That handkerchief didn't smell like it."

"And you say the dishes were empty?"

"That's right."

"Nothing left?"

"Clean as a bone."

"The men must have been hungry then?"

"Well, in taking a dinner out that way, you can't carry too much. You can't carry soup, and water, and all that stuff. You're luck to pile the grub on the dishes, and get it there while it's still warm. People don't eat as much in a restaurant as they think they do. That's because we bring them crackers and butter and go off and leave them for a while, and they munch on crackers. Then after a while, we bring them soup, and then we leave them alone, then bring them bread and butter. They don't start eating the main order until anywhere from ten to twenty minutes after they sit down, sometimes half an hour. It depends on the crowd?"

"You mean you can't wait on them as rapidly when there's a crowd?"

"No," the witness said, "that's when we *do* wait on them. When there's a crowd, it means the restaurant is losing money every time anyone finds the joint filled and goes away. So we always try to shovel the grub into the customers so we can clear out the tables. When business is slack, restaurants figure it's a poor ad to look barren and deserted with just one or two people eating. So then we stall the customers along, and hold them just as long as we dare. That way people coming along the streets look in through the windows, and see a pretty fair crowd, and figure it's a good place to eat."

"In other words," Mason said with a grin, "regardless of our own convenience, we customers are held as living advertisements when we enter a restaurant during the slack time."

"Well, customers make swell window dressing if that's what you mean," Baker said.

"That's what I mean," Mason told him affably. "Thank you."

"The next witness," Kittering announced, "will be William Bitner."

Bitner proved to be a handwriting and fingerprint expert who qualified himself as an expert in his profession, and started the long routine of introducing exhibits, photographs of latent fingerprints found upon doorknobs, bureau drawers, table tops, glassware.

Time droned on endlessly while the tedious process of identifying each photograph went on. Then when the photograph had been introduced, handed to counsel for inspection, and received as an exhibit, it was necessary to wait while the court made the necessary identification; and then the process went on again. Kittering, with a mind which reveled in detail, paused to make sure that the exhibits were properly numbered in numerical order.

When he had finished with some forty-two exhibits, he started exploding his bombshell, a bombshell which was legally powerful, yet which lacked dramatic force because of the long, drawn-out manner in which the details had been dragged through the record. "I show you a card containing ten fingerprints, and ask you who took the imprint of those fingerprints," Kittering said.

"I did," the witness answered.

"When did you take them?"

"Three days ago."

"Where did you take them?"

"In the county jail."

"And what are they?"

"Those are ink impressions made from the ten fingers of the defendant in this case. Those fingerprints are grouped into pairs in accordance with the accepted practice, and reduced to a fraction. That is, a number, representing certain figures used for classification, appears in the numerator, and another number, similarly taken, in the denominator."

138

"Now then, I will direct your attention to People's Exhibit C, and ask you if on this exhibit appears a fingerprint similar in any way to any of the ten prints shown on this card."

"Yes, sir."

"Where?"

"Here, to the side of the bureau drawer. You will note the prints of the middle finger of the right hand. I have here an enlarged copy of that print, together with an enlarged copy of the print of the middle finger of the defendant's right hand. I detected twenty-three points of similarity."

"Will you please explain to the court these points of similarity."

And so the afternoon droned on with the state remorselessly piling up an avalanche of fingerprint evidence against the defendant, with Alden Leeds sitting erect and dignified, without so much as batting an eyelash, Perry Mason and Della Street, fighting against the sheer fatigue of inaction, yet with nothing to which they could object, listening to the legal bricks being dropped into place in a wall which was designed to cut off all hope of the defendant's escape.

At length, the hour came for the afternoon adjournment.

"How much longer will you be with this line of evidence, Mr. Deputy District Attorney?" Judge Knox asked.

"Probably all day tomorrow, Your Honor."

"Very well, court will reconvene at ten o'clock. In the meantime, the prisoner is remanded to the custody of the sheriff."

As court adjourned, Mason moved over to place a reassuring hand on Alden Leeds' shoulder. His face, which was turned toward the courtroom, was wreathed in a confident smile, but the low-pitched words which came from his lips, and were only audible to the ears of the defendant, were far from reassuring. "It looks as though you'd been holding out on me," Mason said.

Leeds faced him calmly. "I am not a young man," he said. "I have but little to gain from an acquittal in this case, and less to lose from a conviction. I didn't realize that I had left fingerprints in that apartment. I did not kill John Milicant. He . . . We can prove he was alive and well when I left."

Mason's eyes narrowed. "We can produce evidence to that effect," he said, his lips still smiling reassuringly, "but that's no sign a jury is going to believe it. One thing is certain. The judge is going to bind you over on a charge of first degree murder."

"I had anticipated that, " Leeds admitted quietly.

"*We* hadn't," Mason observed. "We would have if you'd told us about these fingerprints."

"I didn't know about them."

"You knew you'd searched that apartment."

Leeds said nothing.

Mason, smiling broadly, patted him on the shoulder as a deputy sheriff approached.

"Okay, Leeds," he said, loudly. "Things are looking fine. They don't have a ghost of a chance of pinning this on you. Get a good night's sleep now, and leave the worry to us."

Out in the corridor, Della Street fell into step with Perry Mason. "Those fingerprints," she said, "don't look so good, do they, Chief?"

"I'd more or less discounted them in advance," he said. "I figured that Leeds must have been the one to search that apartment, although he said he hadn't. What I was mainly counting on was that he'd been too smart to leave fingerprints. Apparently, he was in too much of a hurry to be careful."

"What," she asked, "would happen if tomorrow they show that his fingerprints are on the handle of the knife?"

Mason shrugged his shoulders. "Let's not worry about that in advance. He's in bad enough right now. Let's go to the office and see if Drake has uncovered anything."

Chapter 12

At the office Mason found a letter addressed to him in feminine handwriting on the stationery of the Border City Hotel at Yuma. The letter read simply:—

DEAR MR. MASON:

   I am a seamstress soliciting work by mail. If you have any sewing which I could do, or if there are any tears or holes which seem hopeless, you will find I am quite skillful, and I will deeply appreciate having an opportunity to show you what I can do. Simply address Mrs. J. B. Beems at the Border City Hotel, Yuma, Arizona.

Mason took out his notebook, made a note of the address, thought for a moment, and then touched a match to the letter.

Della Street, who had gone down to Drake's office to notify him that Mason was back, came in with the detective in tow. "Hi, Paul," Mason said. "What's new?"

Drake jackknifed himself into a characteristic pose in the big chair, and said, "I've located Inez Colton."

"Where?" Mason asked.

"At the Ellery Arms Apartments," Drake said. "She's used henna on her hair and is going under an assumed name, but I don't know what name, or the number of her apartment. I was afraid to make any inquiries without consulting you, for fear she'd get wise and take another powder. You see, Perry, I can't put a tail on her because we have no one who knows her personally, and no one to put the finger on her. We simply have a description to go on."

"How did you ever locate her?" Mason asked.

"Simple," Drake said. "Like all other good gags, it's been used before, but it's one of the things people seldom think of. I figured she'd try to change her appearance. Walking out on her job that way indicated it. I managed to find out who her favorite hairdresser was, and an operative, posing as a friend and doing a lot of talking, got the information out of the hairdresser—at least that much information. Women hate to have strange hairdressers do a dye job."

Mason pushed his hands down deep into his pockets. "I wish we had a little more on her before we make the contact," he said.

Drake said, "I can help on that too, Perry. You can prove that Jason Carrel is her boy friend all right."

Mason's eyes lit up. "That smug liar," he said. "He had the crust to get on the witness stand and swear absolutely that there had never been any conversation among the relatives about what it would mean to them financially if they could keep Alden Leeds from marrying or making a will. He adopted the position that he was radiating sweetness and light. He just wanted to help his poor, dear uncle, and that was all he thought about."

"What did he say about Inez Colton?" Drake asked.

"Swore he didn't know her."

Drake grinned and produced a photostatic copy of a traffic ticket. "All right," he said. "Let him try this on his piano. Here's a traffic ticket showing a violation of the parking law—car parked between the hours of two A.M. and four A.M. The license number is that of Jason Carrel's automobile, and after the citation was issued, a cute little trick showed up at the traffic department and paid the fine. Her name was Inez Colton. She wanted a receipt showing that the fine had been paid in cash. That's rather unusual. The bail clerk made a notation on the traffic ticket. When I had him look it up, he found the receipt stub showing payment by this Colton baby."

"This was the night of the murder?" Mason asked, excitedly.

"No, no," Drake said. "This was two weeks before the murder. I had a tip the car sometimes stood out in front of the

142

apartment house until the small hours of the morning. So I went up and checked through the traffic violations on the off-chance I might find something. I did."

Mason said gleefully, "Hot dog! Wait until I slap him in the face with that and ask him how it happens that Inez Colton is paying the fines on his traffic citations. He claimed he didn't know anything about her, had never seen her in his life."

Mason pocketed the photostatic copy, and said, "Let's eat, and then go call on Miss Colton, and see what she has to say. Della, you can take a shorthand notebook. Work as inconspicuously as possible, take down every word of the conversation."

Della Street said, "Gosh, I'm too excited to eat."

"Let's go to the Home Kitchen Cafe," Mason said. "We can get a good square meal there."

"Expense account?" Drake asked.

"Expense account," Mason said.

At the Home Kitchen Cafe, they were waited on by the same waitress who had waited on Mason at lunch the day he had interviewed Serle. "Heard anything from Hazel?" the lawyer asked.

"Not a word," she said. "No one's heard anything."

"Come on," Drake said. "Let's order."

Della picked up her menu. The waitress said, "If you like the daily special, I'd recommend it—unless you want a short order."

"Let's see," Della said, studying the menu. "What's today?"

"Friday," Drake snorted. "What a gal!"

"Friday," Della said. "Well, I'll take the fish special."

Mason looked at the menu. "The roast lamb, for me," he said to the waitress.

"Same here," Drake told her.

"Do you," Mason asked of Paul Drake, "have a correspondent in Yuma?"

Drake nodded. "There's an agency there that will take over."

Mason took a pencil from his pocket, turned the menu over, and wrote on the back of it, "Mrs. J. B. Beems, Border City Hotel, Yuma, Arizona." He slid it across to the detective, and said, "Don't repeat this out loud, Paul. Just remember the name and address. I want a damn clever operative put on that party."

Drake read the name on the menu. "I can," he said, "get someone on the job down there by telephone, and then can send down a clever woman operative to take over in the morning. She's sixty-five, white haired, motherly, and could talk blood out of a turnip.—Well, what I mean is, *listen* blood out of a turnip. You know the type, Perry."

Mason said, "That would be swell."

The waitress appeared with large bowls of steaming soup, and Mason, folding the menu so she couldn't see the name on the back, shoved it down into his pocket.

They ate hurriedly and for the most part in silence. When they had finished, Drake said, "Gosh, Perry, I don't know why any man would want to get married when restaurants serve meals like this."

"*You* wouldn't," Della Street said.

"Ouch!" Drake observed, laughing.

Mason called the waitress, handed her a bill, and said, "Bring the gentleman over there half a dozen packages of gum."

"What flavor?" she asked.

"Spearmint," Drake said.

"What brand?"

"I don't care, just so it's gum."

When she had gone, Mason said, "You have to admit, Paul, Leeds makes a good host."

Drake said, "Well, a two-bit cigar would have been equally acceptable."

The lawyer shook his head. "You're going calling on a lady," he said. "A cigar on top of this dinner would make you feel at peace with the world, generous, kindhearted, and impulsive. I want you to be your own sweet self, nervous, gum-chewy, and deceptive."

Drake said, "Well, come on then. Let's go and get it over with."

"How," Della Street asked, as they drew up in front of the

apartment house, "will you find out what apartment she's in, Chief?"

Mason said, "Oh, that's routine to Paul. Just let him worry about it."

Drake said, "Let's go," and led the way up to the entrance of the apartment house.

Mason pressed the button marked "Manager" and, a moment later, an electric buzz announced that the latch was released. The three pushed their way into an ornate little lobby, across from which a mahogany door bore the legend, "Manager." Drake crossed and rang the bell. A few moments later, a tall, thin woman who had once had fire and charm in her wide brown eyes inquired, "Did you wish an apartment?"

"No," Drake said. "We're collecting a bill."

The cordiality left her face.

"One of your most recent tenants," Drake went on, "is a girl who's been here before and ran up a bunch of bills. She's about twenty-five, good figure, recently used henna on her hair, big, limpid eyes . . ."

"She hasn't been here before," the manager said. "She's new."

"How long have *you* been here?"

"Two years."

Drake frowned and said, "We're from the Credit Bureau. My memo is that she was here about eighteen months ago under the name of Doraline Sprague."

"Well, that's not the one."

"What name's she going under now?"

"Her own."

Drake said impatiently, "Well, let's have it, if we're on the wrong track, we want to know it."

"Helen Reid."

"What's her number?"

"Twelve B."

"What floor?"

"Second floor."

Mason said, after the manner of one pouring oil on troubled

145

waters, "Why don't you go and have a frank talk with her, Paul? After all, the bill isn't large. You don't want to make a mistake. A lawyer will cost you money, and cause her a lot of trouble. You might make her lose her job."

Drake hesitated.

"Go ahead. Talk with her, Paul," Della Street pleaded. "I'm satisfied that's the only way."

"What's the use of talking with her?" Drake said. "She'd lie out of it. We've got all the stuff we need. Let her prove she isn't the one. I think she is."

"I'm not so certain, Paul. Come on, let's talk with her."

Drake heaved a sigh. "Okay," he surrendered reluctantly.

Mason flashed a reassuring smile at the manager. "Personally," he said, "I think it's a mistake."

They took the stairs, starting to climb leisurely, running up them two at a time as they got out of sight of the manager. Mason said, "Hurry, Paul. She may telephone, and let her know we're on the trail."

They trooped down the corridor.

Drake said to Della Street: "Tap on the door, Della. If she comes, all right. If she doesn't, and wants to know who's there, remember you're the girl from across the hall, and you're out of matches."

They paused in front of the door. Della Street tapped gently on the panel. After a moment of silence, a woman's voice said, "Who is it please?"

Della said gushingly, "Oh, I'm from across the hall, and I've run out of matches. My boy friend's been working late, and I'm making a pot of coffee and some scrambled eggs. I'll only need just a couple."

The door opened.

The young woman who stood on the threshold was striking in appearance. The henna hair did not particularly become her, but the limpid, dark eyes, the very red, full lips, the smooth lines of her neck stretching down into perfectly formed curves visible beneath the sheer silk of the lounging pajamas, gave her a somewhat voluptuous appearance; while the dead white of

146

her skin, drawn tight across the forehead and wide cheekbones, made her seem peculiarly exotic.

Drake and Mason took charge without giving her an opportunity to collect her thoughts or take any independent action.

"Okay, Inez," Drake said, pushing his way into the room and taking care not to remove his hat. "The jig's up."

Perry Mason tilted his own hat a little farther back on his head and nodded.

Della Street glanced about her in swift appraisal, taking in little details which only a feminine eye would observe.

Drake dropped into a chair, crossed his long legs, lit a cigarette, and said, "So you thought you could get away with it, eh?"

Mason said, "Now wait a minute, Paul. Let's give her a break. Let's hear her side of the story before we do anything rash."

"Hear her side of the story!" Drake exclaimed scornfully. "She walks out of her apartment, tries to disguise her appearance, takes an assumed name. I suppose all that was just because her delicate nerves couldn't stand the idea of living in an apartment house where a man had been murdered."

"You don't think *she* did it, do you, Paul?" Mason asked.

"Her boy friend did," Drake said, with the complete detachment of one who is discussing a problem which holds no personal interest for him.

Inez Colton said indignantly, "This is an outrage! What do you mean by tricking me in this way? You said you wanted matches."

"Forget it, sister," Mason said. "I'm trying to do you a favor. This guy," indicating Drake with a sideways gesture of his head, "is hard. If you don't think he's hard, just cross him. I claim you didn't know what you were getting into, that you were in love, and that it's up to us to give you a chance to come clean before we do anything drastic."

"What do you mean—drastic?" she asked, and there was a slight quaver in her voice.

Drake laughed scornfully.

Mason said, "Now listen, Paul, let's be fair about this thing. She *may* not have been mixed up in that murder."

"Then what did she run away for?"

"To protect her boy friend, of course."

"Well, you know the law. If she gives aid to a murderer to shield him, she becomes an accessory after the fact. And how about this talk Milicant had over the telephone . . ."

Mason said, "Now wait a minute, Paul. I'm going to be firm about this. You're not going to condemn this young woman until we hear her side of the story."

Mason turned expectantly to Inez Colton.

For a second or two, it seemed that she was on the point of rushing into swift speech. Then her eyes became hard and suspicious. She seemed to lower a veil over her thoughts. "What do you want?" she asked.

Mason said, "The truth."

"I have done nothing wrong."

"Come on, come on," Drake said. "Let's have it."

Mason said, "Shut up, Paul. I'm going to insist that you have a chance to tell your story, Inez."

There was doubt in her eyes. She glanced appealingly at Della Street, then said, "Well . . ."

As she hesitated, Drake said, "We have a witness who saw Jason Carrel when he left your apartment, so there's no good trying to cover up."

She whirled to face Drake. Her eyes narrowed slightly. Her muscles became poised, tense. "Jason Carrel leaving my apartment?" she asked.

"That's right," Drake said.

"Who are you and what do you want?"

"I'm a detective," Drake said.

"Well, you're barking on the wrong track, Mr. Detective. Jason Carrel was never in my apartment. I see it all now. You two are trying to run a bluff, figuring you'll get me to talk. Thank you. I have nothing to say."

Mason said, "Suit yourself," and handed the subpoena to Paul Drake.

148

Drake, crossing over to her, said, "Under those circumstances, you get a subpoena to appear in court tomorrow morning at ten o'clock and testify on behalf of the defendant in the case of the People versus Alden Leeds."

"But I can't come to court. I mustn't."

Drake shrugged his shoulders, "That's *your* funeral, sister."

"But I don't know anything that would help anyone. I know nothing whatever about that murder."

"Save it for the witness stand," Drake said.

"All right, I will," she said defiantly, "and don't think my testimony is going to help Alden Leeds any, because it won't."

"What do you know about Alden Leeds?" Drake asked.

"That's none of your business. Put me on the witness stand, and I'll tell."

Drake said conversationally, "Too bad about Jason Carrel. He said he didn't know you. Unfortunately, he was testifying under oath in a murder trial, and a court reporter took down what he said."

There was a triumphant glitter in her eyes. "Put me on the witness stand," she challenged. "I dare you!"

Abruptly, Mason, who had been watching her carefully, said, "I'm afraid, Miss Colton, that you're getting a wrong impression. Mr. Drake isn't very familiar with the various Leeds relatives, and apparently he's made the mistake of confusing Jason Carrel with Harold Leeds. . . . What you mean, Paul, is that Harold committed the murder."

Inez Colton winced as though Mason's words had been a physical blow. Consternation showed in her eyes. She said, in a stammering half whisper, "He . . . told me . . . you didn't know."

Mason's low laugh was filled with calm confidence. "He *really* thought that?" he asked. "It's what we wanted him to think, of course, until we had him trapped. That's why I refrained from asking Jason Carrel whether he had loaned his car to his cousin."

"Then you're . . . you're Perry Mason, the lawyer who's representing Alden Leeds?"

Mason nodded.

"You can't pin it on Harold."

Mason said patiently, "*We're* not pinning anything on anyone—but Harold can never convince a jury he didn't do it."

She said, "Harold went downstairs to see him, and he was dead."

"Went alone?" Mason asked.

"Yes."

"And told you he was dead?"

She nodded, in tight-lipped silence.

"Why didn't you notify the authorities?" Mason asked.

"As far as that's concerned, why didn't Alden?"

"*I'm* asking about *you*," Mason said conversationally.

"For the very good and sufficient reason that we couldn't afford to mix into it. We didn't think anyone knew. How did you find out?"

Mason said, "Finding out things is our business, Miss Colton. Don't you think you'd better make a complete statement?"

Della Street, who had unobtrusively slipped her shorthand book from her purse and taken notes of the conversation, now shifted her position so that the notebook rested on the arm of the chair.

"There's nothing to tell. I . . . We . . ."

She broke off as a gentle tapping sounded on the panels of the door. Without making any move to answer, she raised her voice and said, "I have nothing to say. Even if you do accuse Harold Leeds of murdering Milicant, you can't . . ."

Mason upset his chair, jumped to his feet and made for the door. Inez Colton screamed.

Mason jerked the door open, said to the figure which was sprinting down the corridor, "Come back here, Harold, and face the music. Running away isn't going to do you any good."

Harold Leeds paused uncertainly, turned a wan, frightened face toward Perry Mason.

"The house is watched, you fool," Mason said. "Come back here and face the music."

A door in one of the apartments opened. A fat, blonde woman

150

with startled eyes stared wordlessly from Mason to Harold Leeds.

"Come back," Mason said. "Don't leave Inez to face the music alone."

Harold Leeds turned and walked slowly back toward Mason.

"Come on," Mason said. "Hurry up. Don't act so much like a dog coming to take a licking. You've played a man's game. Now face the results like a man."

Harold Leeds glanced appealingly at the blonde woman in the doorway who was regarding them with startled, curious eyes. It was as though he hoped someone would come to his rescue, that he might wake up and find it was all a horrible nightmare.

As Leeds came closer, Mason took his arm, escorted him to the door of Inez Colton's apartment. Drake was sitting very much as Mason had left him. Inez Colton was in the chair, sobbing quietly. Della Street had changed her position slightly so that her raised knee partially concealed the shorthand notebook.

Drake said conversationally, "Figured you could handle the situation out there, Perry. Thought I'd better keep an eye on the one here."

"Oh, Harold," Inez Colton said tearfully. "*Why* did you do it? You promised you wouldn't come near me."

Harold Leeds said sullenly, "Gosh, Inez, I made absolutely certain no one was following me. How did I know I was going to walk into *this* guy?" indicating Mason with a jerk of his head. "I simply *had* to see you."

Mason said, "Suppose you tell us all about it, Harold. Sit down where you can be comfortable, and get it off your chest. You'll feel better then."

"I have nothing to say," Harold Leeds said, "particularly to *you*. If I talk, it will be to the district attorney."

"That's swell," Mason said. "But first, young man, you'll go on the witness stand as a witness for the defense. I'll ask you why you went downstairs to John Milicant's apartment, what your business dealings with Milicant were and why you deemed

151

it necessary to kill him. You can answer those questions on the witness stand. Here's a subpoena."

With a flourish, Mason handed him a subpoena to appear as a witness for the defense in court at ten o'clock A.M. the next day. The young man, as one in a daze, extended a quivering hand to take the folded oblong of legal-looking paper.

Mason said to Paul Drake, "Okay, Paul, let's go. Come on, Della. We have nothing more to do here."

Leeds said, "Wait a minute. You can't . . . can't put me on the witness stand."

"You just *think* I can't," Mason said.

"No! No! You can't! I wouldn't help your case any. I'd hurt it, and I can't afford to get mixed up in this thing."

"Why not?" Mason asked.

"Because . . . because I can't."

"That's too bad," Mason observed without sympathy, starting toward the door.

Inez Colton straightened in the chair. "Oh, go ahead and tell him, Harold," she said. "What's the use of trying to lie out of it now."

Then, as Harold remained sullenly silent, she said to Mason, "All right. *I'll* tell you if *he* won't. Harold's crazy about the ponies. He can't keep away from them. Neither can I. I'm a married woman. I was married to a man who was a race track tout. We knew John Milicant, but we knew him as Louie Conway, a plunger. I met Harold out at the race track. I was having a squabble with my husband. Harold and I fell in love. I decided to leave my husband, and wanted some place to live where he'd never find me, because he's just the type to make trouble. I spoke to Louie Conway, and asked him if he couldn't get me a job. He could and he did. I took an apartment in the same building where he had an apartment. I went under the name of Inez Colton. Harold started calling on me, and one day he and Louie ran into each other in the elevator. Harold recognized Louie as John Milicant. Louie, of course, recognized him as Harold Leeds. That was all there was to it. Louie told Harold to keep quiet about what he knew. He was afraid his sister was

152

going to find out what he was doing. Then when Harold found out that Alden Leeds had made a big check in favor of L. C. Conway . . . Well, Harold thought he should do something about it. Louie told him to come down and talk things over.

"Harold went down to his apartment.

"Milicant told a most amazing story. He said that he was actually entitled to a full one-half of all of the money Alden Leeds had ever made, that Alden Leeds secured his original start by stealing one-half of his fortune, that it all went back to the time when Leeds was in the Klondike, and . . ."

Mason, his eyes glinting with interest, said, "Are you, by any chance, going to say that Milicant claimed he was Bill Hogarty?"

Her face showed surprise.

"Yes," she said, "that's exactly what he did say and showed documents to prove it."

"Where are those documents now?" Mason asked.

"I don't know."

Harold Leeds said sullenly, "He *was* Hogarty all right."

"And Emily Milicant is his sister?" Mason asked.

"She's no more his sister than I am," Inez Colton said. "Up there in the Yukon, Leeds took possession of the cabin and all the grub. He beat up Hogarty and then drove him out of camp at the point of a gun, without blankets, without food, and, as he thought, without matches. Then Alden Leeds took all the gold, and mushed out to civilization. He was shrewd enough to take the name of Hogarty, making it seem that Leeds had been the one to disappear. That threw the authorities off the track. Hogarty almost died of cold and exposure. Leeds had hit him a terrific blow on the head in the fight which preceded his being driven out of camp. The fight was over Emily Milicant who had been Hogarty's sweetheart. She was a Dawson dance hall girl.

"Hogarty decided not to complain to the authorities. He made up his mind he could let Leeds think him dead, that then, after Leeds had grown careless, he would track him down, and force an accounting.

"Leeds went to Seattle, met Emily Milicant, told her Hogarty

153

was dead, and married her. He married her under the name of Hogarty. Then, in some way, Leeds found out Hogarty was on his trail, and ran away—vanished into thin air, leaving his wife behind him. The real Hogarty found the wife. There was an argument, of course, a period of hot words and accusations, then they made up. They lived together as man and wife for some time, then finally broke up, but remained good friends. She wanted to find Leeds. Hogarty wanted to find him and force an accounting. They finally discovered him. Leeds had again taken his real identity when he thought there was no further danger. That's the way Hogarty told the story to Harold, the way Harold told it to me."

Mason turned to Harold Leeds. "Is that," he asked, "the truth?"

"That's the truth," Leeds said.

"What did you do?"

"What could I do? My hands were tied. Apparently, it was a matter between Hogarty and Uncle Alden. Hogarty said that Uncle Alden was willing to make out a settlement."

"And you went down to see Milicant, or Hogarty or Conway, whatever you want to call him, the night of the murder?" Mason asked.

"Yes," Harold Leeds said, in a voice which was almost inaudible.

"What time was it?"

"Right after Uncle Alden left."

"How do you know?"

"I saw Uncle Alden leave the Conway apartment and walk down the corridor to the elevator."

"Where were you?"

"I was coming down the stairs. The stairs are back toward the end of the corridor. I'd just reached the foot of the stairs when the door of the apartment opened, and Uncle Alden walked down the corridor to the elevator. He was moving very rapidly."

"You didn't speak to him?"

"No."

"Why not?"

"He seemed—well, nervous and upset—and I couldn't explain to him about Inez. I didn't want him to know I was . . . there in the building."

"So what did you do?"

"After he'd gone down in the elevator, I went to the Conway apartment."

"Knock on the door?" Mason asked.

"The door was slightly ajar, an inch or so. I knocked on it. There was no answer. I pushed the door open, and called Conway's name. He'd asked me never to call him Hogarty, and not to refer to him as Milicant while he was there in that apartment. There was still no answer. The apartment had been searched. Papers were scattered about. There were some empty dishes on the table. Evidently, two people had eaten a hurried dinner, and . . ."

"Why hurried?" Mason asked.

"Because places weren't set at the table. The plates were placed just as they'd been left, with the knives and forks dumped on the tray. There was a pot that had contained coffee on the tray and two saucers. The cups were dirty."

"The dishes weren't piled up?" Mason asked.

"No, left just as though people had eaten hurriedly and dropped the dishes back into place."

"And the knives and forks were on the tray?"

"Yes."

"You evidently looked that over pretty carefully."

"I did. I wondered if Uncle Alden had been eating dinner with Conway because—well, I thought Uncle Alden had broken in and stolen those papers Milicant—Hogarty—had."

"You say there was a pot of coffee?"

"The pot had contained coffee. You could smell it."

"There wasn't any left?"

"No, not a drop."

"Any food left?"

"No. The plates were slick and clean."

"No bread, no butter?" Mason asked.

"Nothing, just the bare plates."

155

"Go on from there," Mason said.

"Well, I looked around the apartment a little, and opened the bathroom door."

"It was closed?"

"Yes, it was closed but not locked."

"What did you find?" Mason asked.

"The body."

"Then what did you do?"

"I stood right there with cold sweat breaking out all over me," Leeds said, talking more rapidly now as he warmed to the story. "Then I realized what a sweet spot *I* was in. I'd messed around there altogether too much. So I took my silk handkerchief, polished off the doorknobs I'd touched, and beat it."

"Did you leave the door open?"

"No. I wanted to delay the discovery of the body as long as possible so we could clear out. I pulled the door shut. The spring lock clicked into place."

"How long was it after your uncle had left the apartment when you went in?"

"Perhaps ten or fifteen seconds, just long enough for Uncle Alden to walk rapidly to the elevator and start down in the cage."

"How long were you in there?"

"Not over two minutes."

"To whom have you told this?" Mason asked.

"Not a living soul except Inez."

Mason glanced significantly at Paul Drake, then looked over to where Della Street, catching up with her fountain pen on the rapid-fire conversation, held her hand poised over the shorthand notebook.

Inez Colton said, "So you see Harold's position. He can't help your client any, Mr. Mason, and his testimony would clinch the case against Alden Leeds."

"You think Alden Leeds did it?" Mason asked, staring steadily at Harold.

"I don't know," the young man said. "I do know that Uncle Alden was raised in a hard school. If Hogarty's claim was justified, I hope Uncle Alden would have done something about it. I like to think so, anyway. But if it wasn't justified, and Hogarty was trying to hold him up, I . . . Well, I don't know just where Uncle Alden would draw the line. I know one thing, I'd hate to have him on *my* trail. Any time you cross Uncle Alden, you have a fight your hands. . . . I think Uncle Alden found him . . . No, I don't know *what* happened."

Abruptly, Mason got to his feet. "Well," he said, "that's that."

"How about this subpoena?" Inez Colton asked.

"Forget it," Mason said. "As far as we're concerned, it hasn't been served. Tear it up."

Harold Leeds shot forth an impulsive hand. "That's mighty white of you, Mr. Mason," he said, "and you can rest assured that I'll keep all of this under my hat."

"Sorry we broke in on you this way," Mason said to Inez Colton. "Come on, folks. Let's go."

Della Street closed her notebook, slipped it back into her purse. Drake glanced sidelong at Mason, then got to his feet without a word. Mason led the way out into the corridor. Inez Colton bid them goodnight and closed the door.

As the three marched wordlessly down the corridor, the fat, blonde woman, who had stood in the doorway when Mason brought Harold Leeds back into the room, opened the door and stood staring silent, expressionless, motionless. She was still standing there when the trio entered the automatic elevator.

"Well," Mason said, on the ride down, "I've played right into the D.A.'s hands. Apparently, Milicant really was Hogarty."

"I thought you knew he was," Drake said.

Mason twisted his lips into a lopsided grin. "I wanted the police to think I thought he was," he said. "Let's get to a telephone where I can put through a long distance call."

"Want me any more?" Drake asked.

Mason said, "No. Get to work and try to plug some of these other loopholes."

"Looks as though you'd bitten off a little more than you can chew, Perry," Drake said, dropping a hand on the lawyer's shoulder. "Take it easy this time. Remember this isn't *your*

157

funeral. If your client's guilty, he's guilty. Evidently he's lied to you. Don't throw yourself into the case and leave yourself wide open."

Mason said, "He isn't guilty, Paul—at least not the way they claim."

Drake said, "Okay, Perry. I'll take a taxi back to the office."

He walked over to the curb, gave a shrill whistle, and sprinted for the corner to stop a cruising cab.

Della Street glanced at Perry Mason. "Well, Chief," she said, "we seem to be taking it on the chin."

Mason said, "There's a hotel in the next block, Della, with a switchboard and telephone booths. I think we can get a call through."

"Whom are you going to call, Chief?" she asked.

"Emily Milicant," he said. "There are some holes I want mended. . . . Evidently she knew there would be."

They walked to the hotel. Mason gave the switchboard operator his call and told her to rush it. "Mrs. J. B. Beems at the Border City Hotel, Yuma, Arizona."

They smoked a silent cigarette. Della Street's hand moved over to grip Mason's arm, a wordless pledge of loyalty. Then the telephone operator beckoned to Mason. "The hotel's on the line," she said, "but they have no such party registered."

"I'll talk with whoever's on the line," Mason told her.

"Okay," she announced, snapping a key on the switchboard. "Booth three."

Mason entered the telephone booth, said, "Hello, is this the night clerk of the Border City Hotel?"

"That's right," a man's voice said.

"I'm anxious to find out about Mrs. Beems."

"We have no one by that name registered here."

"You're certain?"

"Absolutely certain."

Mason said, "I received a letter from her, stating that she was registered there under that name and would stay there until she heard from me. She's heavy around the hips, thin in the face, with big, black eyes. She's around fifty, although she could pass

158

for forty-two or forty-three, medium height, with black hair, talks with a quick, nervous accent, and keeps her hands moving while she's talking."

"She isn't here," the night clerk said. "This isn't a large hotel. We only have three unescorted women, none of whom answer the description—and it happens we know something about all three. One of them has been here a year, one going on to three months, and the other two weeks."

Mason said, "Okay, thanks a lot. Sorry I bothered you," and hung up. He crossed over to the switchboard operator, paid the toll charges, left her a dollar tip, and said, "Come on, Della. Let's go."

Out on the street, she said, "Chief, what does it mean?"

Mason, frowning, reaching in his pocket for a cigarette, offered no explanation.

"Suppose the district attorney should get hold of Harold Leeds?" Della Street asked. "We found him, and why couldn't the D.A. find him? After all, we've given them the lead by dragging Inez Colton into it."

Mason's reply was an inarticulate grunt. He shoved his hands down deep into his trousers pockets, lowered his chin to his chest, and slowed his walk until it was a slow, even, regular pace. Della Street, accustomed to his moods, slowed her own steps and remained silent.

Abruptly, Mason said, "Okay, Della. We stick in our stack of chips. If we hold the low hand, we're wiped out."

"Chief, why mix yourself into it?" she asked. "After all, Leeds is just a client, just the same as any other client. If they can prove him guilty, it's not your fault. He undoubtedly lied when he said he left Milicant alive. Apparently, Milicant really *is* Hogarty, and the sister's given you a double cross. You're certainly not called on to do any great amount of worrying. Let them come clean with you. Sit back and simply act as a lawyer, presenting a case."

Mason grinned. "I can't," he confessed.

"Why not, Chief?"

"I don't know. I guess it's the way I'm built. Come on, Della. We're going to put in a call."

He took her elbow, piloted her into a drugstore, crossed to the public telephone, and dialed police headquarters. "Homicide Squad," he said, and, after a moment, "Sergeant Holcomb, please. . . . Hello, Sergeant? Okay, here's a hot tip for you. Harold Leeds, a nephew of Alden Leeds, was in Milicant's apartment the night of the murder. He saw his uncle leave the apartment, and go down the hall to the elevator. He entered the apartment right after his uncle, and found Milicant dead. Inez Colton, his girl friend, knows all about it. She skipped out after the murder because she didn't want to be involved. She's living under the name of Helen Reid at the Ellery Arms Apartments. Harold Leeds is there now."

Sergeant Holcomb's voice was excited. "You're certain?" he asked.

"Absolutely," Perry Mason said. "I know the whole business."

"Fine," Sergeant Holcomb exclaimed. "If this tip proves on the up and up, you'll get the thanks of the department. Who is this talking?"

Mason said, "You know me well, Sergeant. I'm a short, fat guy with whiskers. I usually wear a long, red coat with a big black belt."

"I don't place you," Sergeant Holcomb said, his voice puzzled.

Mason said, "Santa Claus, you damn fool," and hung up.

Chapter 13

The long table ran the length of the visitors' room in the county jail. On each side of this table, chairs were grouped. Dividing the table, running lengthwise along it, and from one end of the room to the other, stretched a meshed screen of heavy wire, extending from the ceiling to the floor. This screen was supported by steel frameworks which contained two doors. Access to the room was through a species of anteroom which was separated from the visitors' room by iron bars. In this anteroom, two men were constantly on guard, a locker, containing riot guns and tear gas bombs, close at hand.

Perry Mason entered the anteroom and presented a pass to the attendant. The attendant scrutinized it, stepped to the telephone, and said, "Send Alden Leeds up." He stamped the pass with a rubber stamp, unlocked a steel door, ushered Mason into one side of the divided room, and locked the door behind the lawyer.

Mason strolled over to one of the chairs, sat down, and lit a cigarette. At that time, there were no other visitors in the room. Morning sunlight, striking the barred windows at an angle, filtered weakly through to form oblong patches of barred shadow on the floor.

When Mason's cigarette was half consumed, a door at the far end of the room opened, and Alden Leeds stepped directly from the elevator into the visitors' room. He saw Mason, nodded, and walked across to seat himself in a chair on the opposite side of the table and on the other side of the screen.

Mason studied the other man's face, a face which was within five feet of his own, separated by a table and a wire screen. It was possible, by leaning on the table, for a prisoner to get his lips within a few inches of the screen, possible for the lawyer on the other side of the screen, to place his ear within a corresponding distance.

Mason, however, made no attempt to lean across the table. Lowering his voice so that it was inaudible to the deputies, who were busily engaged working with their books, Mason said, "Well, Leeds, in an hour court opens. In order to represent you, I ought to know where I stand."

Leeds sat quietly, with none of that nervous fidgeting which so frequently characterizes a prisoner. The morning sunlight showed the pouches under his eyes, the calipers which stretched from his nostrils to the corners of his mouth, the seamed skin which had been cracked in Arctic frosts, baked by tropical suns. His eyes were cool, steady, and cautious. "What," he asked, "do you want?"

"I want the truth."

Leeds said, "You have the truth."

Mason, hitching sideways in the chair, crossed his long legs in front of him, and said, "The way I figure it, you learned that Milicant and Conway were the same. You entered the apartment to find Milicant dead. You knew there was going to be hell to pay unless you could find the documents which you knew, by that time, Milicant had in his possession. You tried your best to find them, and finally had to give it up as a bad job.

"It wasn't a time when you were at your best. The thing had hit you right between the eyes. You knew what you were up against, and the knowledge didn't help to steady you. When you realized you couldn't find what you wanted, you became more frenzied in your search."

"Thanks," Alden Leeds said.

"For what?" Mason asked.

"For not thinking that I killed him. I was afraid you would."

Mason said, "Your fingerprints are all over the place. A witness saw you leaving the apartment. He stepped into the apartment right after you'd left. He found evidences of a search and . . . "

"Where was John Milicant?" Leeds asked.

"Apparently lying in the bathroom dead."

"This man didn't look?"

"No."

Leeds shrugged his shoulders, and said, "I'm not trying to tell you your business, Mason. You're a lawyer. I'm not."

Mason said, "If you hadn't lied to me at the start, I might have thought so, too. But I don't think we can put that across with a jury now."

Leeds accepted the statement philosophically. "Too bad," he observed.

Mason nodded. "Isn't it?"

There was a moment of silence. Then Mason said, "The warden up at San Quentin doesn't care particularly about capital punishment. He carries out a death sentence when he has to, as part of his duties of office. He claims that new gas chamber is worse than the rope."

Leeds turned cold, frosty eyes on the lawyer. "Are you," he asked, "by any chance trying to frighten me with the idea of death?"

Mason, meeting his glance, said simply, "Yes."

"Don't do it," Leeds commented. "It won't work."

Mason, watching the man's calm face, let his own features soften into a smile. "I was afraid of that," he admitted.

After a moment, Leeds said, "All right. Let's begin from there."

Mason said, "The way I figure it, Emily Milicant killed Hogarty. You were away from the cabin at the time. She must have dusted out in a panic. You tried to overtake her, and couldn't. Then, you did the best you could to cover up evidences of what had happened and . . . "

He broke off as Alden Leeds' face twisted into writhing expression.

"You weren't looking for that one, were you?" Mason asked conversationally.

For a moment, Alden Leeds seemed to be fighting for his self-control. But when he spoke, his voice was calm and well-modulated. "No," he admitted. "I wasn't. You're smarter than I'd figured."

Mason said, "The worst of being an attorney is that you're obligated to protect your clients. Sometimes your clients don't want to be protected. They get chivalrous and try to take a rap. Then it's up to the lawyer to go ahead and protect them anyway."

Leeds said, "Look here, Mason. This is sheer nonsense, but it's dangerous nonsense."

Mason said, "Emily Milicant has taken a run-out powder. She sent me a phoney letter from a Yuma hotel, hoping that would pull the wool over my eyes."

"She isn't there?" Leeds asked, his voice either showing surprise or a well-simulated imitation.

"No," Mason said. "That hotel has no party by that name stopping there—no one at all who answers the description."

Leeds digested the information in thoughtful silence.

"Suppose," Mason said, "you tell me a little more about Hogarty."

"Suppose I don't?"

"In that event," Mason said, "I'll fill in the gaps as best I can, and do as I see fit."

"What makes you think Emily killed him?"

"Lots of things, " Mason said. "I don't think you're the type who would run away from a killing in a fair fight, and I don't think you'd kill a man deliberately unless you did it to protect someone you loved. If you'd done that up in the Yukon, there'd have been two witnesses—you and Emily. You'd have stayed and faced the music."

Leeds twisted his long fingers together. "Emily," he said, "was high-spirited. She was fond of adventure, and the restrictions which were carried over as an aftermath of the gay nineties, didn't appeal to her in the least. She went very much on her own. She was very willful, very determined, and very independent."

"Go on," Mason said.

"She'd met Hogarty. She came up to the claim as a young

woman who wanted to throw in her lot with two prospectors on a basis of share and share alike. She was willing to do her share of the work to make the cabin neat and attractive, to do the cooking, to do anything else she could around the mine. But she wasn't going to stand for some of the stuff Hogarty had in mind. Hogarty overplayed his hand when I was in at the nearest settlement getting grub. I came back and found her gone. She'd left a note."

"Where's that note?" Mason asked.

"Burnt," Leeds said crisply.

"She killed him?"

"Evidently," Leeds said. "They had a knockdown and drag-out battle. Emily shot, and the bullet knocked him over. He got up and ran out. She didn't know where he was hit. It was toward the end of the season. It was getting dark early. I think it was the trail of the blood on the floor and in the snow that put her in a panic. She threw some things onto a sled, and started out. There were only two dogs left in camp. I was getting provisions with the big dog team."

"When did you get back to the cabin?"

"Three days later."

"You tried to find her?"

Leeds nodded. Evidently, he didn't care to discuss that phase of the matter.

"And you tried to find Hogarty?"

"Hogarty was dead," Leeds said. "He'd been shot in the abdomen. Another prospector took care of him. That prospector's name was Carl Freehome. I, of course, didn't know that until later. I got there to the shack, found it deserted, found Emily's note. We'd struck it rich while we were working on a pocket. That had been before Emily showed up. We didn't let Emily know. Hogarty refused to let her in on that. The gold was cached under the floor of the fireplace. I dug up the gold, used the provisions I'd got as a stake, and made it through to White Horse. I found no trace of Emily.

"Then was when I had the idea of throwing the authorities off the track by going out as Bill Hogarty. Then if anyone accused

165

her of murdering Bill Hogarty, the records would show that he'd left the country. If they claimed it was Leeds she'd murdered, Leeds could show up very much alive and well. It was the best I could do for her under the circumstances."

"You finally found her in Seattle?"

"Yes."

"When did you hear about this man Freehome?"

"I didn't hear about him. She did years later. She told me a few weeks ago when we met. I employed a detective agency to try to find him. The said he'd been seen two years ago in Dawson City. There, they lost his trail. Later on they heard a rumor he was in Seattle."

"What became of Hogarty's body?"

"After he died," Leeds said, "Freehome loaded it on his sled, went up to the cabin. He found the hole where I'd dug the gold cache out of the floor, and was shrewd enough to tell that it had been a pretty good cache. He started looking around, and found the rest of the pocket. Lord knows how much was left in it. I wasn't interested at the time. I was trying to find Emily. . . . That's my theory anyway, putting two and two together from the facts as I discovered them.

"Put yourself in Freehome's place. It was a wild country. Winter was coming on. The ground was freezing up hard. Freehome had a chance for a stake. He dug a shallow grave, buried Hogarty, and went to work. When he'd finished with the claim, he left Hogarty where he was. He had no other choice. Legally, the claim was ours. He'd stripped it of the rest of the pocket. Naturally he didn't want to have an argument over who owned the gold. . . . I wanted to find him and tell him he could keep the gold—if he had any left. What I wanted was his story. I hoped that Hogarty had made some statement before he died. That's why we flew north."

"You didn't find him?"

"Lord, no! We didn't have a chance to even look. The police nabbed me first."

Mason said, "Your nephew, Harold, apparently has been cutting a wider swath than he's been given credit for. His mistress had an apartment in the same building with Milicant. Leeds went downstairs to call on Milicant. He'd found out Milicant was going under the name of Conway, and found out about the twenty grand. Harold didn't know whether it was blackmail or what. He wanted to find out. He's the witness who saw you leave the room."

"Harold, eh?"

"It doesn't seem to surprise you," Mason said.

Leeds said dryly, "Nothing surprises me. I've had too many birthdays."

"I don't suppose," Mason said, "that, under the circumstances, you'd care to go on the witness stand and tell your story."

Leeds looked at him, steadily, slowly shook his head.

Mason scraped back his chair, and got to his feet. One of the deputy sheriffs reached for the telephone. Mason said, "I'll see you in court," and walked across to the barred door. The second deputy opened the door, escorted Mason through the anteroom, and out into the corridor. Leeds, standing behind the screen of the divided table, turned to wait—expectantly facing the door of the elevator which was to take him down to the jail.

Drake was waiting for Mason at his office. It needed but a look at Della Street's face to tell Mason that the detective had bad news. "What is it, Paul?" he asked.

Drake said, "We've located Emily Milicant."

"Where?"

"San Francisco."

"What's she doing there?"

"Hiding out in a hotel."

"Anyone with her?"

"Uh huh."

"Who?"

"Ned Barkler."

"Oh, *oh*!" Mason said. He slid his weight to the corner of the desk and lit a cigarette. "Together?"

"In the same hotel, but not living together."

"How come?" Mason asked.

"Well, when you told me that she'd taken a powder on you and wasn't in Yuma, we started checking airplanes. She'd been in Yuma all right, and probably mailed you the letter telling you she was going to the Border City Hotel, but after she did that, she went to the telegraph office and asked for messages for Mrs. J. B. Beems. She got a message. We don't know what it was. Anyway, she took a plane for San Francisco as soon as she read the telegram. Barkler was waiting for her there."

"They're still there?" Mason asked.

"No," Drake said. "That's the bad part of it. The police located her about the same time my men did."

"The same time," Mason echoed.

"Uh huh," Drake said. "To me, Perry, it stinks. I think *my* telephone line has been tapped. It looks as though they've moved in on us. Every move we make is being watched."

Mason's face darkened. "By God," he said, "I'll bust those guys wide open!"

"I didn't know my line was tapped. I've got the lowdown on yours," Drake went on. "There was a stakeout where your telephone conversations were being recorded on dictaphone cylinders. We located the room. One of the men left there, and my operatives shadowed him. He's a detective working under Homicide out of headquarters. You know what that means, Perry. They're closing in on us."

Mason said, "By God, they can't pull that with me. I'll find out who's responsible for this and start turning on the heat. They . . ."

"They don't care now," Drake interrupted. "They've closed the net. They took Emily Milicant and Ned Barkler into custody, and are bringing them back."

"On what charge?" Mason asked.

Drake said, "I don't know, perhaps material witnesses, perhaps as accessories after the fact. They're gunning for you, Perry, and they're using big caliber guns. You know what they'll do to *me*."

Mason said grimly, "But they don't know what I'll do to them! Right now I could put Emily Milicant on the spot. If I had

168

to, I could just about convict her of the murder of Bill Hogarty, and by letting the D.A. prove Milicant was Hogarty, I could rip their case wide open."

Della Street said eagerly, "Are you going to do it, Chief?"

Mason, staring moodily at the carpet, shook his head.

"Why not?" she asked.

"Just an old-fashioned custom," Mason said, "—one that's almost out of date—that of shooting square with a client."

Chapter 14

Court convened at ten o'clock.

Late spectators, shuffling into the courtroom, looking in vain for seats, were admonished by a stern bailiff that there was to be no standing room, that only seated spectators could remain. The low-pitched hum of buzzing conversation, the rustling of restless motion on the part of the spectators, combined to furnish a back-drop of sound, against which the whispered conversation of Perry Mason and Della Street blended so perfectly that only their postures showed they were holding an important conference.

"Gertrude Lade understands her part?" Mason asked.

Della Street nodded.

"Did she make any objection?" Mason asked.

"Not a bit," Della Street said. "She seemed to like the excitement."

Mason grinned. "Guess she hired out to the right party."

"I'll say she did," Della Street said.

A side door opened, and a deputy sheriff escorted Alden Leeds into the courtroom.

The whispered conversation died to a dead silence, broken only by the breathing of the attentive audience, a breathing which was a sequence of overlapping sounds, without rhythm.

Judge Knox entered the courtroom from his chambers, and the bailiff rapped the court to order.

Bob Kittering, struggling to keep his voice calm as he arose from his chair, said, "If we may have the indulgence of Your Honor, the prosecution would like to remove the fingerprint expert from the stand long enough to interrogate a new witness

170

who knows important facts which were not entirely within the possession of our office yesterday."

Judge Knox glanced at Perry Mason.

"No objection," Mason said.

"Very well, so ordered," Judge Knox observed.

Kittering said, "Call Harold Leeds to the stand."

Harold Leeds moved forward from the rear of the courtroom. His steps lagged as though his legs recognized all too clearly the nature of the ordeal awaiting at the end of their journey.

"Step right up," Kittering said. ". . . That's better . . . Hold up your right hand and be sworn. Now give your name, address, and occupation to the clerk. Be seated on this witness chair. . . . Now, Mr. Leeds, your name is Harold Leeds. You are a nephew of the Alden Leeds who is on trial here in this action as a defendant. Is that right?"

"That," Harold Leeds said moodily, and with his eyes downcast, "is right."

"Were you acquainted with John Milicant prior to his death?"

"I was."

"Did John Milicant, at any time, tell you anything concerning his true identity?"

"Yes, he did."

"What was it?"

Judge Knox said, "Just a minute before you answer that question," and looked down at Mason as though expecting an objection. When he heard none, he said, "I'm not certain, gentlemen, but what this question plainly calls for hearsay evidence."

Kittering pulled his brief case toward him, and took out several pages of closely-written, legal foolscap.

"If Your Honor will permit me," he said, "I would like to be heard on this. While it is true that the question may, in one sense of the word, call for hearsay evidence, in another sense of the word, it is the sort of hearsay evidence which, by law and custom, has been universally accepted in all courts of justice.

"For instance, the question is frequently asked a witness,

171

'How old are you?' And the witness replies, giving his age. Obviously, the question calls for hearsay evidence, and the answer is founded on hearsay. Yet, it is universally accepted as being necessary in the nature of things that such an exception to hearsay evidence should be permitted.

"Now we come to another and similar situation. A man establishes his identity by going under a certain name. If a man goes under a certain name, that is all that is necessary to establish at least a *claim* to identity. In the present case, we propose to show that the decedent went for many years under the name of Bill Hogarty, that it was under this name, he met and prospected with Leeds in the Yukon. . . ."

"I understand," Judge Knox said, "but this question asks the witness to repeat something which the decedent told him. It is your contention that this is part of the *res gestae*?"

"Yes, Your Honor."

Judge Knox frowned. "I'm going to reserve a ruling on that question for the moment," he said. "The court is inclined to think that there should be some foundation in the case for supporting the contention that this is a part of the *res gestae*."

"I was trying to show that it was, by this very question, Your Honor."

"I understand that," Judge Knox said patiently, "but I think you had better first lay a foundation so that the court can determine intelligently how much of a time factor is to enter into the determination of the *res gestae*."

"And," Kittering pointed out, in a sudden burst of inspiration, "there's no objection on the part of counsel for the defense."

Judge Knox's face showed a flashing expression of surprise. He glanced down at Perry Mason, frowned, and said thoughtfully, "I guess that's right. Do I understand, Mr. Mason, that such is the case?"

Mason said, "Such is the case, Your Honor. There has been no objection."

"Well," Judge Knox said irritably, "lay some foundation anyway."

Kittering said, "I will ask you this question, Mr. Leeds. Did you, during his lifetime, know a Bill Hogarty?"

"Well," Leeds said hesitantly, "I knew a Bill Hogarty, alias Conway, alias Milicant."

"How did you know he was Hogarty?"

Leeds said, with what evidently was the manner of one reciting by rote, "In the same way that I know you are Mr. Kittering, the deputy district attorney—because he told me so. He told me his name wasn't Milicant, that he wasn't the brother of Emily Milicant, that he was Bill Hogarty, a man whom Alden Leeds thought he had murdered. He said he'd had his nose broken since and put on a lot of weight, and Uncle Alden hadn't recognized . . ."

"Just a moment," Judge Knox interrupted. "I think that answer has gone far enough. The answer, as given, most certainly answers the question, as asked. I think any statement made by the decedent to this witness for the purpose of showing motivation, malice, or bad blood between the parties should not be admitted in evidence unless it is shown that it was a dying statement. And I take it, counselor, your question didn't call for such a communication?"

"No, Your Honor."

"Very well. Proceed."

"Did you see the defendant on the night of the murder—the seventh of this month?"

"Yes."

"When?"

"At about ten-twenty-five in the evening."

"Where?"

"Emerging from the room of Bill Hogarty—or John Milicant, whichever you want to call him."

"Please state exactly what you saw and exactly what you did," Kittering said.

Leeds told Judge Knox his story. At times, his voice was so low that even the court reporter had difficulty in hearing it. At times, he spoke more freely. Always he tried to push into the background his relationship with Inez Colton.

173

When he had finished, Kittering, evidently hoping to take Mason as much by surprise as possible, said abruptly, "Cross-examine."

"That," Mason said with a suave smile, "is all. I have no questions."

Leeds seemed nonplused. The deputy district attorney was frankly incredulous. "Do you mean to say there's to be no cross-examination of this witness? You aren't cross-examining on the question of identity?"

"No," Mason said.

"Very well, the witness is excused, and I will now call one more witness slightly out of order—Mr. Guy T. Serle."

Judge Knox looked down at Perry Mason. "Any objection, counselor?" he said.

"None whatever," Mason said.

Serle came slowly forward, was sworn, answered the usual preliminary questions, and then glanced expectantly at Kittering.

"You knew William Hogarty, alias John Milicant, alias Louie Conway, in his lifetime?" Kittering asked.

"I did."

"You saw him on the evening of the seventh of this month?"

"I did."

"Where?"

"At his apartment."

"When?"

"Some time around half past seven or quarter to eight in the evening."

"Who was present?"

"Just Conway—that is, Hogarty—and myself."

"How long were you there?"

"Until around twenty minutes past eight."

"What happened at that time? Just tell the court what was said and what was done."

"Well, Conway . . ."

"I think," Kittering interrupted, "that in view of the proof which we now have available, it will be better, for the sake of the record, if you refer to him as Hogarty."

174

"Very well. Hogarty and I had had some business dealings. He'd sold me a business. Police had raided it. I figured it was because of a squawk from one of Louie's customers or from someone who was gunning for Louie. I told him I thought it was on a tip-off from Alden Leeds. Louie didn't seem at all surprised. I wanted Louie—Hogarty—to stand back of me. He said he would."

"Was there any other conversation?" Kittering asked.

"That was the substance of it. Hogarty was interrupted by a lot of telephone calls, and he hadn't eaten any dinner and neither had I. He told me to call a number that he gave me and order a dinner. I put in the call and the dinner came up. It wasn't Louie—Hogarty—who called. I did the telephoning. I guess it was right around ten minutes past eight when the dinner arrived. We were both in a hurry and we ate fast. Then I shook hands with Hogarty and left."

"Wasn't there some other conversation?" Kittering asked.

"Oh, yes. He told me to call back at ten o'clock, and he'd let me know if things were okay."

"At what time?"

"Ten o'clock."

"You're certain of that?"

"Absolutely."

"Did you call him back?"

"I did."

"When?"

"At ten o'clock on the dot. He told me things were okay, that he was to have a conference in about ten minutes and that he expected the conference would take about ten minutes, that he'd be free after that and would be sitting right there waiting for my call."

"What time did you call him?" Kittering asked.

"At ten o'clock exactly."

"Cross-examine," Kittering flung triumphantly at Perry Mason.

Mason said, in a tone of voice which was that of an ordinary, informal conversation, "You felt that Alden Leeds had given the officers the tip which resulted in a police raid on your place of business?"

"I figured that was possible."

"And Milicant—or Hogarty, whichever he was—also figured that way?"

"Well, he admitted it was possible. We knew Leeds would be gunning for Conway, trying to get him out of the way—only Leeds didn't know Conway and Milicant were the same, and he hadn't recognized Milicant as Hogarty. He thought Hogarty was dead. Hogarty said he was going to get Leeds in and tell him he was Conway."

"Did you have any trouble getting Milicant to agree to come to your rescue?"

"None whatever. He recognized that it wasn't fair to make me the goat in his business."

"Did your troubles affect your appetite?" Mason asked.

"My appetite?"

"Yes."

"No. When things go against you, they go against you. That's all there is to it. There's no use pulling a baby act."

"Isn't it a fact that in the Home Kitchen Cafe on the eighth of this month at some time during the lunch hour, you intimated to me that if Alden Leeds would give you some form of financial renumeration, you would change your testimony so it would appear that telephone conversation with Conway took place *after* Leeds had left Conway's apartment?"

"That's not true," the witness shouted, "and you know it's not true!"

"You made no such offer?"

"No. You tried to bribe me and I told you Alden Leeds didn't have money enough to make me change my story. You tried to threaten me, to bribe me, and to intimidate me."

Judge Knox regarded Mason in frowning concentration, but Mason casually passed on to something else.

"Mr. Serle," he asked, "you were arrested the night of the murder on a felony charge, were you not?"

"Yes."

"Have you ever been prosecuted on that felony charge?"

Kittering was on his feet. "Objected to as incompetent, irrelevant, and immaterial," he said. "It is not a proper question by way of impeachment. It is only when a witness has been *convicted* of a felony that that point can be brought out on cross-examination."

Mason said, "I am not trying to impeach the witness. I am trying to show bias."

"Objection overruled," Judge Knox said.

"I haven't been tried on that case," Serle said, "because there wasn't any case. The raid was made on a tip-off from Alden Leeds. There wasn't any evidence."

"As a matter of fact," Mason said, "you were shrewd enough to realize that you could ingratiate yourself with the district attorney's office by changing the time of that telephone conversation from ten-thirty to ten o'clock, and did so. Now isn't it a fact that this telephone conversation which you have referred to as taking place at ten o'clock actually did not occur until approximately thirty minutes later?"

"That is *not* a fact," Serle shouted.

"And that as you first related that conversation to the officers at headquarters and as you subsequently related it to me there in the Home Kitchen Cafe, you made no mention of Hogarty telling you that he had a conference in ten minutes which he expected would take about ten minutes?"

Serle shifted his position, but his voice was calm. "I remembered some of the conversation more clearly after I'd had a chance to think it over. But that's what Hogarty told me all right. . . . You know how those things are. You don't remember everything a man says to you over the phone the first time you try to recall the conversation."

"After you left this apartment house where Conway, or Milicant, had his apartment, you went directly to the All Night and Day Pool Room, did you not?"

"No."

"You didn't?"

"No."

"How long was it after you left Conway's apartment before you entered the pool room?"

"I don't know. I'd say it was fifteen or twenty minutes."

"And what were you doing in the meantime?"

"Various things."

"Name one."

"I was telephoning."

"To whom?"

"A friend."

"Who was this friend?"

Serle paused and looked expectantly at Kittering. Kittering got to his feet, and said, "Your Honor, I object. Not proper cross-examination. Counsel can be given a reasonable latitude in checking the time element. Please note that so far as this witness is concerned, there is no question whatever of his testimony being pertinent to the case except insofar as it relates to the question of time. It is the contention of the defense, naturally, that this telephone conversation occurred *after* Leeds had left the apartment. It is the contention of the prosecution that it did not."

Judge Knox glanced down at Perry Mason. "I'd prefer to have you pass this question for the moment, counselor, and lay some foundation to show that it's pertinent to the case. The court doesn't want to embarrass other parties by dragging in their names—unless it's necessary."

Mason went on with the cross-examination, calmly, casually. "Isn't it a fact that when you entered the pool room, you told witnesses there that you were going to call Louie Conway around ten-thirty?"

"I may have," Serle said.

"You were lying to these men?"

"I wasn't lying. I saw no reason for telling pool-room loafers all of my private affairs."

"Notwithstanding the fact that you knew when you entered the pool room that you intended to call Bill Hogarty, or Louie Conway, as the case may be, at ten o'clock, you nevertheless

178

told these men that you were going to place the call at somewhere around ten-thirty?"

"Yes."

"Didn't you tell the district attorney when you first repeated your story that you had called Conway at ten-thirty?"

"No."

Kittering said, "Your Honor, I would like to have the decedent referred to as Hogarty rather than Conway. It will keep the record free from confusion, and . . ."

Judge Knox interrupted. "There is not sufficient proof as yet to warrant the court to require counsel to so frame his questions."

Mason said, as though the point were of no great importance: "Oh, I guess it's all right. I'll stipulate his real name was Hogarty, and so refer to him if counsel wishes."

"Very well, so stipulated," Kittering said.

Judge Knox looked sharply at Perry Mason. "That stipulation of identity may be important on the question of motivation, counselor."

"It's all right," Mason said carelessly. "I've known he claimed to be Hogarty for some time, and if Kittering has proof of it, I'll save time by stipulating."

"I do have proof," Kittering said.

"Very well," Judge Knox observed. "Go on with your cross-examination, Mr. Mason."

"Did you tell the district attorney at first that the time was ten o'clock?" Mason asked.

"I didn't mention any time."

"I see," Mason said. "You told the officers that you had called Hogarty. They then explained to you that it was important to fix the time of that call because if it was after ten-twenty, it would mean they couldn't convict Alden Leeds of the murder. Isn't that right?"

"Well, we had a talk. They told me some things and I told them some."

"Did they explain to you the importance of the time element

before you mentioned the exact time of that telephone conversation to them?"

"Well, yes."

"And you were shrewd enough to realize that this might give you an advantage, so you made some statement to the effect that you saw no reason why you should co-operate with the officers if they were going to raid your place of business, and arrest you on a felony charge, did you not?"

"Well, naturally, I didn't feel any too cordial."

"And one of the officers said that that might be fixed up, didn't he?"

"Well, he said that if the prosecuting witness didn't show up, it was no skin off their shins."

"All right," Mason said, "now getting back to what you did after you left Hogarty's apartment. You telephoned a friend of yours. Isn't it a fact that that telephone call was to the Home Kitchen Cafe, and that you talked with Hazel Stickland?"

Serle's face showed alarmed dismay. "Why . . . I . . ."

"Remember," Mason said, leveling a rigid forefinger at him, "you're under oath."

"Well, yes. I did call her, but not at the cafe."

"And what did you tell her?"

"Objected to as incompetent, irrelevant, and immaterial, and not proper cross-examination," Kittering said.

"Sustained," Judge Knox ruled. "You may fix the time of the conversation, counselor. The subject matter would seem beyond the scope of proper cross-examination."

"Your Honor, I think this conversation is pertinent," Mason said.

"I don't, not as the question is asked at the present time. You are, of course, the cross-examiner, and, therefore, have the right to ask leading questions. If you think the conversation is pertinent, frame a question to show that fact."

Mason, turning to Serle, inquired, "Isn't it a fact that you told Hazel Stickland to pack her things, and leave town, that you would meet her, give her some money, and explain?"

"Same objection," Kittering said.

Judge Knox frowned at Perry Mason. "Is it your contention, counselor, that this has anything to do with the crime?"

"Yes," Perry Mason said. "This girl was a waitress at the Home Kitchen Cafe, and was quite friendly with this witness. On the night of the murder, Serle located Bill Hogarty, *before* Hogarty went to his apartment. He took Hogarty to the Home Kitchen Cafe for dinner, Hazel Stickland waited on them. The restaurant had two 'specials' for dinner that night. One was filet of sole and baked potatoes, the other roast lamb chops, peas, and baked potatoes. Serle and Hogarty had the meat dinner. . . . I have here a menu from that restaurant showing the regular weekly dishes."

"What time was this?" Judge Knox inquired, puzzled.

"Approximately six o'clock or six-fifteen," Mason said.

"But this witness had dinner in the apartment with Hogarty the night of the murder," Judge Knox pointed out. "There seems to be no question of that fact."

"Look at his face if you think he did," Mason said.

Kittering was on his feet. "I object to this colloquy between court and counsel, and I object to that statement on the part of counsel. I assign it as prejudicial misconduct."

Judge Knox glanced swiftly at Serle's white, drawn face, then looked back to Perry Mason. "The objection is overruled," he said. "Answer the question."

"Isn't that a fact?" Mason asked. "Isn't that what you told her?"

"No," Serle said, in a strained, harsh voice.

"You tried to get Hogarty to come through with bail. He wouldn't come through," Mason said. "You knew that even if you were bailed out, you'd never be allowed to reopen your business. You were furious. You paid him money for that business. You demanded a return of the purchase price; and you also insisted that he must put up bail. He refused. You started brooding. You knew that he had the better part of twenty thousand dollars in his possession, probably on his person in a money belt. After you separated, you began to wonder whether it would be possible for you to murder him and get that money,

181

but do it in such a way that you would have a perfect alibi. You knew something about how autopsy surgeons fix the time of death from the extent to which digestion has progressed. You knew that at six-fifteen, Hogarty had eaten, and exactly what he had eaten.

"Almost two hours later, you went to his apartment, and killed him. You paused long enough to order a restaurant in the block to bring you up food that was exactly the same as that which Hogarty had consumed in the restaurant. When the waiter arrived with the food you were in Hogarty's bedroom, apparently engaged in a spirited conversation with him . . . but Hogarty was already dead. You were pitching your voice to two different tones, and doing all the talking yourself. Isn't that right?"

"It's a lie!" Serle shouted, his voice was strained and hoarse.

Mason went on calmly and remorselessly. "You waited until the plates had arrived, and then scraped all of the contents of the plates into the garbage chutes."

"I did not."

"Then you left, intent upon building up an alibi. You were careful to see that the door was locked. You didn't know Marcia Whittaker had a key to that apartment. You left there after the murder and went to the pool room where you knew you could find several of your cronies, and took occasion to tell them that you were going to call Hogarty at around ten-thirty.

"Then, to clinch matters, and make it appear that the decedent had been murdered right after that telephone conversation, you pretended to dial the number and talk with him on the telephone. You pretended to be engaged in a conversation about bail. And from the pool room you went directly to the police station, figuring that that would be the safest way for you to clinch your alibi."

"I did nothing of the sort," Serle said with dogged persistence.

Kittering, who had recovered his composure, said, "Your Honor, I object to this. This is an attempt to browbeat the witness. It . . ."

182

"Objection overruled," Judge Knox said. "Proceed, Mr. Mason."

"Better think again," Mason said, "because I'm going to prove what I say, Serle."

Serle clamped his lips tightly together, and said nothing, but the skin across the top of his forehead began to glisten as it slimed with cold perspiration.

"Now," Mason went on calmly, "let's go back to the night of the murder. You went to the Home Kitchen Cafe. Hazel Stickland waited on your table. She . . ."

"I didn't eat there the night of the murder," Serle blurted. "I ate with Hogarty in his apartment. I tell you, I never was at the Home Kitchen Cafe any time that night."

Mason said, calmly, "You were there, Serle. You and Bill Hogarty. You may have arranged to get rid of the waitress, but you perhaps failed to notice that two girls were seated at the table next to you, and that Hogarty was surreptitiously trying a pickup."—Mason whirled abruptly to face the audience. "Miss Gertrude Lade," he called out. "Will you stand up please?"

Gertrude Lade stood up.

Mason, pointing a rigid forefinger, said, "Look at that young woman, Serle. I am going to ask you if you have ever seen her before—if, as a matter of fact, she wasn't seated at the table next to you when you were eating dinner in the Home Kitchen Cafe on Friday, the seventh of this month?"

Gertrude Lade said, "That's him all right."

The deputy district attorney jumped to his feet, spouting objections. Mason held up his hand, and said, "No, no, Miss Lade, not a word from you! *Please!* Your time will come later, you and the young woman who was with you. I just wanted to ask Mr. Serle to identify you, that's all. Sit down please."

Gertrude Lade sat down.

Serle's face had turned a pasty green.

At that moment, the door of the courtroom opened, and two deputies escorted Emily Milicant into the room.

Mason met her eyes in a stony stare, whirled suddenly to face Serle once more. "You still insist that you ate dinner in the company of Bill Hogarty in his apartment and not at the Home Kitchen Cafe?" Mason asked.

Serle hesitated a moment, then blurted, "We ate two dinners. Once there and once in the apartment. He was still hungry."

Mason smiled. "And were you so hungry," he asked, "that you ate up everything off the plate?"

"Yes."

"You want this court to understand that you ate the jackets from the baked potatoes?"

"Yes," Serle said. "I always eat them."

"And," Mason observed, "you also swallowed the bones from the chops, did you not?"

Serle's eyes stared at Mason in speechless fear.

Mason said, "You'll have to try and do better on your next murder, Serle. When you scraped the plates down the garbage chute, you made a fatal error in neglecting to remember that it is customary to leave bones on the plates."

Mason smiled affably at Judge Knox, and said, "It is the contention of the defense that when Alden Leeds arrived at the apartment, Hogarty was dead. It is, I presume, true that Milicant was really Hogarty. He had been blackmailing this defendant, and it was only natural, although perhaps not legally proper, for the defendant to try and regain possession of papers which he knew were in possession of the dead man, papers which would make public the very disclosures he had sought to suppress. And so the defendant searched the apartment—which accounts for his fingerprints. He made a frantic effort to find those papers."

"But," Kittering countered, jumping to his feet, "those papers were papers which connected him with the attempted murder of Bill Hogarty, with the stealing of his property, and . . ."

"Oh, no," Mason said with a smile. "*Those* papers related to an entirely different matter. The defendant found them, thank you. They have been destroyed."

And Mason sat down.

Serle yelled, "It's a lie!"

Kittering said, "Your Honor, I object to . . ."

Mason whirled to face Kittering, "If you were a little more interested in finding the *real* criminal, and a little less in trying to convict an innocent man, merely because you have started to prosecute him, you'd be cooperating with me in this thing instead of opposing me. . . . When the first check was given to Hogarty, the bank had to cash it, but, thinking it might be blackmail, they wrote down the numbers on the bills. Serle got those bills after the murder of Hogarty. I think you'll find them in his possession right now."

Judge Knox said, "This court is going to take a twenty-minute recess. We . . ."

He broke off as Serle, shouting, "I refuse to stand for this persecution," streaked across the courtroom and through the door of the judge's chambers.

Judge Knox shouted at the deputy sheriff, who had Leeds in charge, "Get him! Get him! Don't sit there like a fool!"

The deputy sheriff sprinted into action.

Mason scratched a match on the sole of his shoe, and lit a cigarette.

Della Street squeezed his wrist enthusiastically. "Chief," she said, "I could dance a jig on the judge's bench."

"Take it easy," he told her. "Be nonchalant. Light a cigarette. Remember people are watching you. Act on the assumption that you can pull a rabbit out of the hat any time any place. How about a cigarette?"

"Give me the one you're smoking, Chief," she said. "I couldn't light a cigarette to save my life. Why did you make that crack about Alden Leeds finding Hogarty dead, and then searching the apartment?"

"Because I wanted to explain his fingerprints," Mason said, "and I wanted to give Emily Milicant a tip on the Hogarty angle. I . . ."

He broke off as Kittering came storming over to their table.

Kittering, his voice so indignant that he could hardly talk, sputtered, "What the devil do you mean . . . You'll be disbarred for this."

"For what?" Mason asked.

Kittering pointed an indignant finger at Gertrude Lade. *"That girl,"* he stormed. "She was no more in the restaurant than I was! One of my investigators tells me she's in your office, working at the switchboard."

"That's right," Mason observed, calmly exhaling a cloud of cigarette smoke.

"You can't pull that stuff and get away with it," Kittering stormed.

"Why not?"

Kittering said, "Because it's illegal; it's unethical; it's . . . I believe it's a contempt of court. I'm going to see Judge Knox, and tell him the whole contemptible scheme."

Kittering strode away in the direction of the judge's chambers. Mason continued to smoke calmly and placidly.

"Chief," Della Street said in a half whisper, "don't you suppose Judge Knox will figure it *is* a contempt of court?"

"I don't give a damn what he figures," Mason said, elevating his heels to the seat of an adjoining chair. "I hope he does. It's time we had a showdown. It's getting so that any time we don't follow the conventional methods of solving a case, somebody wants to haul us up before the Grievance Committee of the Bar Association. To hell with them! It's time they learned where they get off."

"But, Chief," she said, "this was . . ."

Mason interrupted her to nod his head toward where the two deputies, who had escorted Emily Milicant into the room, were engaged in a low-pitched conversation with Alden Leeds.

"Look at them," he said. "They're pulling the same old tactics. They're telling Leeds that Emily Milicant has confessed to everything, and that there's no use trying to hold out any longer. They think *they* have the right to pull any of this third degree stuff, that if *we* do it, we're shysters. To hell with that stuff. I . . ."

He broke off as Judge Knox, his face grave, appeared at the door of his chambers and spoke to the bailiff. The bailiff crossed over to Mason, and said, "The judge wants to see you in his chambers immediately, Mr. Mason."

Mason ground out his cigarette, and said, "Wait here, Della. If anyone asks you anything clam up on them. Don't talk, and above all don't try to explain."

Mason strolled on into the judge's chambers, heedless of the babble of excited voices which filled the courtroom, of the curious eyes which followed him.

Judge Knox said, "Mr. Mason, Mr. Kittering has made a charge of such gravity that I feel I should call on you for an explanation before taking any steps. If this charge is true, it is perhaps not only a contempt of the court, but a flagrant violation of professional ethics."

Mason seated himself comfortably, crossed his legs, and said, "It's true."

"You mean that this young woman was planted in the courtroom for this purpose, that she is an employee of yours, and was not at the restaurant?"

"That's right," Mason said, and then added, after a moment, "There's been a lot of loose talk around here about what constitutes professional ethics. I'm glad to have a showdown."

"You won't be so glad if the court considers it contempt," Judge Knox said grimly.

Mason said, "It's about time the courts realized that they're agencies for the administration of justice. They're instruments of the people. They're here, not to unwind red tape, but to administer justice. I'll admit my cross-examination was irregular, but what's wrong with it? I asked Gertrude Lade to stand up. She stood up. I asked Serle if he didn't remember this young woman as having been at the table next to him. If he'd been telling the truth, he could have said, 'no,' that she couldn't have been there because he wasn't at the table, and that was all there was to it."

"But you had this young woman swear she was there," Kittering protested.

"I had her do nothing of the sort," Mason said, glancing contemptuously at the excited deputy. "In the first place, she wasn't under oath. In the second place, all she said was, 'That's him.' Obviously, it was. He's never claimed to be anyone else. I could

187

point at Judge Knox, and yell, 'That's him.' It wouldn't be a falsehood. He is him. He's he, if you want to be grammatical."

"I don't agree with you," Kittering said.

"All right," Mason said. "We'll debate the point. You take the side that he isn't he. I'll say he is. Now, what proof have you to offer?"

"That isn't what I meant," Kittering said.

"It's what you said," Mason observed.

"Well, you know what I meant."

"I don't give a damn what you meant," Mason commented. "I'm talking about what was said. That's all Gertrude Lade said. She said, 'That's him.'"

"Well, you know what you intended her words to mean."

Mason sighed. "She said it was him. I still contend that it was him. Dammit, it *is* him! I'll go into any court on any contempt proceedings, or otherwise, and insist that it's him. Serle is Serle. That's all she said:—'It's him.'"

Judge Knox's face softened somewhat. The ghost of a twinkle appeared at the corner of his eyes.

Mason followed his advantage. "I have a right to ask anyone in the courtroom to stand up and then point that standing person out to a witness when I'm asking a question. Try and find some law which says I can't."

Judge Knox regarded Mason with thoughtful eyes. At length, he said, "Mason, your mind is certainly not geared to a conventional groove. However, as a matter of justice, I am inclined to agree with you, and I don't know but what I am, as a matter of technical law."

Mason said, "Why not? If we'd followed this case along conventional lines, Alden Leeds would have been bound over on that fingerprint evidence. He might have been convicted."

"He had no right to lie about it," Kittering said.

"He didn't lie," Mason observed. "He kept quiet."

"Well, he should have told us."

"That," Mason said, "involves another difference of opinion. However, the law at present says he doesn't have to. If you have any objection, you'll have to change the law."

188

"He should have notified the authorities as soon as he discovered the body."

"What makes you think he discovered the body?" Mason asked.

"You said he did."

"*I* wasn't under oath," Mason observed.

"But you were acting as his attorney."

"That's right. But you can't convict a man of a crime because of a statement his attorney has made. As a matter of fact, Leeds had never told me that he discovered the body. I'd never asked him that question in those specific words. I merely commented on what *I thought* had happened, in order to assist the court in arriving at a decision."

Judge Knox smiled. "It may interest you to know, counselor," he said to Kittering, "that they caught Serle in the corridor. I don't want to suggest to you how you should conduct your office, but if I were a deputy district attorney, I certainly would strike while the iron was hot, and try to get a confession from him."

"I'll do that," Kittering said savagely. "But I object to these damnable tactics."

Judge Knox frowned.

Mason said, "You tapped my telephone line and listened in on confidential . . ."

"That isn't the point," Kittering interrupted. "The point is, that you tried to trick that . . ."

"What I did was perfectly legal," Mason cut in, "but tapping our line was manifestly illegal. However, you close your eyes to that. Because you were getting something on me, you were perfectly willing to overlook the manner in which the evidence was obtained. You wouldn't have known anything about the dead man being Bill Hogarty unless you'd taken advantage of information received through tapping my telephone line. If *I'd* tapped anyone's telephone line or hired a detective agency to do it, you'd have had me arrested and instituted disbarment proceedings."

"Occasionally," Kittering admitted to Judge Knox, "we have

189

to condone certain irregularities in order to combat criminal activities. It's a case where the ends justify the means."

"The ends in this case," Mason observed, "would have been the conviction of an innocent man of first degree murder."

Kittering jumped to his feet. "You," he said, "can't . . ."

"I really think, counselor," Judge Knox interrupted, "that you should get busy and start discharging the real duties of your office."

Mason smiled across at Judge Knox. "The attitude of the prosecution," he said, "is that they don't care so much about who committed a murder as about keeping me from winning a case."

"That's not true," Kittering shouted.

Judge Knox fastened him with a stern eye. "It seems to be true," he observed, and then added, "If your office has been listening to privileged communications over a tapped wire, it would seem that *your* position is definitely precarious. You understand, counselor, that if Alden Leeds had been guilty, the situation might have been different. Leeds' innocence, however, puts your office in an entirely different position, and puts Mason in a different position, legally, ethically, and morally."

"Some day," Kittering flared, "Mason will defend a guilty man, and then . . ."

Mason yawned, and said, "Well, if counsel doesn't care to confide his discussion to the present, and wishes to neglect the duties of his office, to waste time in idle speculation on the future, I'd like to ask him what he thinks about railroad stocks as an investment . . ."

Kittering flung himself out of the door.

Judge Knox stared across at Perry Mason. "You have to admit," he said, "that you skate on pretty thin ice, Mason—how long have you known Serle was the guilty party?"

"Not very long," Mason admitted. "I should have known it a lot sooner than I did."

"Why?"

"Well," Mason explained, "it's this way. Right from the first, the evidence showed dinner had been ordered at the Blue and

190

White Restaurant, not in the usual manner, but in a most extraordinary manner. In other words, they didn't ask the waiter what was on the menu and then make a selection. The waiter was told to get lamb chops, green peas, and potatoes, and if he didn't have them available, to get them. Then again, the evidence showed right from the first that the plates were empty. It's unusual for two men who are engaged in a hurried conference to order a dinner in that manner. It's unusual for two men to both order the same thing. It's unusual for men to clean up everything on the plates, and it's absolutely unique for a man who has been eating a lamb chop to devour the bone. And you'll remember the waiter testified that the plates were bare. Nothing remained on them.

"Moreover, it's always been my idea that when a man has an iron-clad alibi in a murder case, it's a very good thing to inspect that alibi closely. While a man who has a genuine alibi can't have committed a murder, nevertheless, a man who has committed a deliberate murder always *tries* to provide himself with an alibi. Serle was the only one involved who had an alibi. It looked iron-clad on the face of it, but alibis should never be taken at their face value.

"It was quite apparent that the dead man had a large sum of cash in his possession. That money disappeared. It would seem, therefore, that at least one of the motives for the crime was robbery. Now Alden Leeds might have killed him because of that blackmail business, but he would never have robbed the corpse—not unless he had done so in an attempt to throw the officers off the trail. If he had done that, he would have been far too cautious to have left his fingerprints all over the apartment.

"I knew that Serle ate regularly at the Home Kitchen Cafe. I knew that they had a weekly menu—that is, each day of the week they featured a special, the same dish on the same day.

"The murder was committed on a Friday. Serle accompanied Conway or Milicant or Hogarty—or whatever you want to call him—to his apartment. They were both smoking cigars. At that time in the evening, a cigar usually represents an after-dinner smoke. And then I suddenly remembered what I myself had

191

eaten at the Home Kitchen Cafe on Friday night—roast lamb, baked potatoes, green peas. And I had the menu that they use week after week to prove I wasn't dreaming! A good chemical analysis would probably show the difference between beef and lamb after the digestive processes have stopped working, but the difference between roast lamb and broiled lamb, never."

Judge Knox said, "Personally, Mason, I think it's a most remarkable piece of detective work, an example of sheer deductive genius."

Mason shook his head. "I'll never forgive myself for becoming so engrossed in the incidental matters.—After all, Judge, that's one thing a detective should guard against. He should never let his attention become so concentrated on the incidental matters that he feels they are other than mere incidentals."

Judge Knox studied him curiously. "What," he asked, "were the incidental matters which so engrossed you?"

"Minor matters," Mason said, vaguely, "interesting but purely incidental."

Judge Knox smiled. "Are you, by any chance, referring to the identity of John Milicant as Bill Hogarty?"

Mason said, "That really was a surprise to me, although I should have appreciated the significance of that clue of the frostbitten foot."

Judge Knox let the smile fade from his lips, although his eyes remained kindly. "Mason," he said, "the proof that Milicant was Hogarty certainly seems rather vague and sketchy. If Milicant had been blackmailing Leeds, and one of Leeds' relatives had called on him for an explanation, wouldn't it have been only natural for Milicant to have used the documents in his possession to substantiate a spurious claim made by way of justification to the nephew that he actually was the Bill Hogarty who had been wronged by Leeds years ago? Wouldn't this be the logical way to fabricate a justification for blackmail?"

Mason's face showed surprise. "That," he said, "is an interesting question."

"And do you want me to understand that you have never given it any consideration?" the judge asked.

192

"Well," Mason said with a grin, "no oral consideration."

Judge Knox sighed. "Mason, I confess to a liking for you. I like the colorful life you lead. I like the dashing way you short-cut the conventional methods. I like your career of adventurous excitement. But has it ever occurred to you that Kittering's prophecy is undoubtedly correct? The time will come when you will find yourself defending a guilty client."

Mason arose from his chair. He saw fit to favor the judge with a grin. "He won't be guilty," he said, "until they prove him guilty."

Knox sighed. "I'm afraid you're incorrigible."

Mason bowed. "Thank you, Your Honor," he said, "for the compliment."

Chapter 15

Mason sat in his office, reading the afternoon paper. The sob sisters had literally "gone to town" on the story. Many of the facts which were set forth had been obtained through an interview with Perry Mason, attorney for Alden Leeds, and the reporters reciprocated this donation of information by singing extravagant praises of the manner in which Perry Mason had solved a puzzling case.

Alden Leeds and Bill Hogarty had been in the Yukon in 1906 and 1907. They had fought over a woman. Hogarty had tried to kill Leeds. Leeds had shot him in self-defense. Hogarty had crawled away into the dark, and when it came daylight, Leeds had been unable to find him. It was a wild country. Leeds had a fortune in gold which he dared not leave. Nor did he dare to leave the country without reporting the shooting. He was trapped. So he took the name of Hogarty and left the country. He married the girl under the name of Hogarty.

But Hogarty had not been killed, despite what the others had thought. He had lain desperately ill in the cabin of an Indian. He had shown great determination in journeying to civilization, seeking revenge. Twice on that trip, he had been near the point of death. When finally he had reached civilization, his foot had become frostbitten, and it had been necessary to remove several of the toes on his right foot.

He had carried on his quest for vengeance. In the meantime, Alden Leeds and his wife had separated. Hogarty finally found the woman, but, because she was legally married and not divorced, he had entered into her life, posing as her brother. Then they had found Leeds.

Emily Milicant had realized she was still in love with him.

Hogarty, posing as Emily's brother, wanted blackmail. Leeds, finding himself in this position, had tried his best to work out some fair settlement with Hogarty. His relatives, recognizing the quick, romantic attachment which had sprung up between Leeds and Emily Milicant, and naturally misinterpreting it, had sought to thwart a marriage by having Leeds declared incompetent.

In the meantime, the implacable Hogarty, under the name of Conway, had built up a lottery business which he had sold to Serle. A disgruntled customer had tipped off the police, thinking to get revenge on Conway, in place of which, the trap had closed on Serle, and Serle, in turn, had made demands on Hogarty. When Hogarty laughed at those demands, Serle planned to get his money back from Hogarty. Not being able to do it, save by resorting to murder, he had planned a deliberate crime which, under ordinary circumstances, he could have committed so as to give himself a perfect alibi. It was the ingenuity of Mason's spectacular courtroom tactics which had punctured that alibi.

Della Street entered Mason's office as he was finishing with the paper. "Alden Leeds, his wife, Phyllis Leeds, and Ned Barkler are in the office, Chief," she said. "The police have just released them."

"Tell Gertie to send them in," Mason said.

Mason smiled genially as they crowded about him, shaking hands, showering congratulations. When the first excitement had died away, and Mason was able to get his callers seated, Leeds said, "Mason, I want you to do everything possible to protect Emily. The authorities have been working on that old murder case. The understanding, by which she was released and under which I was released, was that if Alaska wanted us, we would still be held to answer on that old charge."

Mason grinned. "Don't you see?" he said. "There isn't any old charge. They can't charge either of you with the murder of Bill Hogarty because Bill Hogarty was killed on the seventh of this month by Guy T. Serle. Here's a press dispatch which says so."

Leeds knitted his frosty eyebrows for a moment in thought, then glanced up at Mason with a smile. "I see," he said. "You apparently managed to kill two birds with one stone."

Mason grinned. "*I* didn't kill 'em," he said. "I resurrected 'em so I could give my clients clean bills of health."

Alden Leeds whipped a checkbook from his pocket. "I have only one way of expressing my gratitude," he said.

Mason nodded. "Fair enough," he said. "And while you're about it, don't forget that it might be well to make some arrangement for Marcia Whittaker. After all, you know, Leeds, you can't take it with you."

Leeds, shaking ink down to the point of his fountain pen, said, "When you see the amount of this check, Mason, you'll realize I'm not trying to."

Mason took the loaded dice from his pocket, rolled them casually across the top of the desk, and watched the figures five and seven show up with amazing regularity.

Ned Barkler gave a dry chuckle. Mason looked up inquiringly.

"Seeing you rolling those bones," the prospector said, "makes me think of something."

"What?"

"Bill Hogarty," he said. "Probably you're wondering why I made a dash to San Francisco—It goes back to something nobody ever inquired about—How I happened to meet Alden Leeds in the first place. It was over a pair of crooked dice."

Alden Leeds blotted the check he had just written, started totaling figures on the stub and said, "Go ahead and tell him, Ned."

"You see," Barkler said, "I knew Hogarty. . . . Met him in Seattle. Got in a crap game when I was a little high, and lost two thousand bucks. Next morning I found out that the dice were crooked. A bartender tipped me off. It took me a while to make a stake to get up to the Klondike, and then I found Hogarty and Leeds were down the Yukon a ways. I took after 'em, found Hogarty, stuck a gun in his belly and made him pay me off in gold dust.

"Well, when I saw this stuff in the paper about Hogarty and

the frostbitten foot, damn me if I didn't get your play right from the start. Emily told me she was going to Yuma and would register in some hotel as Mrs. Beems; that she'd call for messages at the telegraph office.

"Well, you know, I've got a couple of toes off on account of frostbite—taken off in Dawson City. I figured maybe Emily could fly up there, locate the doctor's records, and claim that Hogarty had also gone under the alias of Barkler. I figured that wouldn't hurt your case any."

He chuckled again. "It would have been a swell game if we could have worked it. Emily got my wire and flew up to San Francisco. Just as we were hatching out the details, in comes the law. . . . Heh heh heh. . . . I was so darned afraid they'd find out about my frostbitten foot that I slept with my shoes on all the time they had me in the cooler. . . . Heh heh heh."

Mason surveyed him with thought-slitted eyes. "You *could*," he said, "state to the newspaper reporters that you knew Hogarty, that he was always a great man to go under an alias, that in addition to Conway and Milicant, he had the crust at one time to go under your name for more than a year."

Barkler puffed thoughtfully at his pipe. "I getcha," he said. "Shortly after that, I take it, I'd sorta disappear, and then those Dawson hospital records would crop up."

Mason said, "When the police walk into a trap by means of wire tapping and listening in on confidential conversations, I always like to give them good measure, crossing the t's and dotting the i's."

Barkler tamped tobacco into the bowl of his pipe with an energetic forefinger. "That detective agency of yours got a man in Dawson they can trust?" he asked.

Mason slowly shook his head. "Not for anything like that."

Barkler grinned across at Alden Leeds. "Well, pard," he said, "I'll be shaking hands now. There's a boat leaves Seattle for Skagway tomorrow afternoon.—And old Ned Barkler would hate to have it said that a lawyer guy had to take a hammer to drive an idea into his head.

"Well, I sort of owe Hogarty one for the trick he played on
197

me with those galloping dominoes. He certainly could handle the bones, that boy, but, hell, he never could have rolled bones all the way from the Yukon down to Southern California like you done.—I've heard of guys killing two birds with one stone, but when one corpse squares two murders—That's what I call a natural! Heh heh heh."

Want to be an expert on Perry Mason?

Then start at the beginning.

THE CASE OF THE VELVET CLAWS

The first Perry Mason novel

by Erle Stanley Gardner

Collect these

ERLE STANLEY GARDNER

titles in colorful, vintage editions . . .

THE CASE OF THE LAME CANARY
THE CASE OF THE HAUNTED HUSBAND
THE CASE OF THE EMPTY TIN
THE CASE OF THE BURIED CLOCK
THE CASE OF THE GOLDDIGGER'S PURSE
THE CASE OF THE LAZY LOVER
THE CASE OF THE LONELY HEIRESS
THE CASE OF THE VAGABOND VIRGIN
THE CASE OF THE DUBIOUS BRIDEGROOM
THE CASE OF THE COUNTERFEIT EYE
THE CASE OF THE STUTTERING BISHOP
THE CASE OF THE DANGEROUS DOWAGER
THE CASE OF THE SUBSTITUTE FACE
THE CASE OF THE SHOPLIFTER'S SHOE
THE CASE OF THE PERJURED PARROT

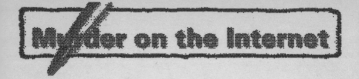